Clarice the Brave

ALSO BY LISA McMANN

THE UNWANTEDS SERIES

The Unwanteds
Island of Silence
Island of Fire
Island of Legends
Island of Shipwrecks
Island of Graves
Island of Dragons

THE UNWANTEDS QUESTS

Dragon Captives
Dragon Bones
Dragon Ghosts
Dragon Curse
Dragon Fire
Dragon Slayers
Dragon Fury

GOING WILD SERIES

Going Wild
Predator vs. Prey
Clash of Beasts

THE VISIONS TRILOGY

Crash
Bang
Gasp

THE WAKE TRILOGY

Wake
Fade
Gone

OTHER BOOKS

Dead to You
Infinity Ring: The Trap Door
Cryer's Cross

Clarice the Brave

LISA McMANN

ILLUSTRATED BY
ANTONIO CAPARO

putnam

G. P. PUTNAM'S SONS

G. P. PUTNAM'S SONS
An imprint of Penguin Random House LLC, New York

Visit us online at penguinrandomhouse.com

Library of Congress Cataloging-in-Publication Data is available.

Printed in the United States of America
ISBN 9780593323373 (hardcover)
1 3 5 7 9 10 8 6 4 2

ISBN 9780593407660 (international edition)
1 3 5 7 9 10 8 6 4 2

LSC

Design by Maria Fazio and Jessica Jenkins
Text set in Maxime Std

To Bill and Chuck, with love.

Mutiny

I'D HEARD THAT word before.

Sailors whispered it on the mess deck, where my brother and I lived in the corner of a wooden crate the color of a November cornfield. They muttered it like an oath late at night after an extra dram of grog. They sent it, quiet, like a prayer, through the ripe silence between slaps of the whip or thuds to the ribs from a thick boot.

I'd heard it, but I hadn't grasped what it meant. Or what it would mean for us.

It was just a word.

OUR CRATE WAS filled with burlap sacks of coffee beans slowly going stale in the locked pantry off the galley. The padlock didn't affect us—we could squeeze under the door easily enough. But it kept out the sailors and the cats. Only Heyu, the pasty-skinned kitchen boy who wore the key on a chain around his neck, came and went several times a day, fetching things for the cook. Nevertheless, we two were safe most of the time, and we had food available. After watching everyone around us die, that's really all we wanted.

My brother, Charles Sebastian, and I were the only ones left of our family. Our siblings had been taken by disease or eaten by Special Lady, who was one of three horrid ship cats. She spent most of her time in the galley near the cook, awaiting a lurch that might cause a scrap of food to fall into her gaping maw. She was the captain's pet: a dreadful, thick orange thing, always trying to sneak into the pantry behind the kitchen boy. She ate our sister Olivia.

Olivia's death had come as a jolt, for she'd been the strongest and fastest of the litter. Her failure to outrun Special Lady weighed heavily on me. If she couldn't survive . . . how could I? Was it only a matter of time? The thought was paralyzing. "How have you made it this long, Mother?" I'd asked soon after, back when she was still with us.

"Some of it was luck, little bean," Mother had admitted. Then she'd examined me carefully, as if able to see the clouds of worry that pressed behind my eyes. "And understanding that hiding can be a better choice than fleeing." After she'd said it, she'd glanced worriedly across the pantry at my brother. Charles Sebastian had an especially strong instinct to run, which led to him sometimes losing his head. The rest of us were constantly trying to teach him how to control his impulses. Was she concerned that he'd be next?

"What if we fail?" I said, feeling faint. "What if we run when we should hide?"

Her warm breath bathed my ear. "Clarice," she said, "when I was young, about to set off alone to see the world, I had a lot of doubts. Leaving my family was hard, but the call of adventure wouldn't stop just because I was scared. On the night I left to stow away on this ship, my father told me something that helped me worry less during the darkest times."

"What was it?" I could hardly get the words out fast enough.

Her sad whiskers, mourning Olivia, turned slightly upward as she remembered. "He said, 'It only takes one mouse to believe in you. And that one mouse is me.'"

I felt a rush of warmth. "And what did you think of that?"

"It made me feel strong, and confident in my decisions. I repeated those words whenever I doubted myself or felt alone in the world." She stared off into the dark pantry, reminiscing. "I can still hear my father's voice . . ." Then she looked at me. "And I want you to know that I believe in *you* as much as my father believed in me."

My mother's sincerity in that moment had made my heart swell. I already knew that I made good decisions most of the time, but her words buoyed my confidence in a way I hadn't realized I needed.

Moments later she'd called Charles Sebastian to go with her on a hunt for fresh water. Perhaps she'd wanted a quiet moment to encourage him in the same way.

We'd never know the answer, though, for on that trip Mother was doused by a rogue wave and swept overboard. Gone in an instant. Charles Sebastian returned alone, shaken to the core. The pantry felt twice its size without her presence to fill it.

My mother loved the sea, but I despised it. Her death gave me even more reason to hate it. Water is deceptive. It seems soft, but it isn't. A wave's unexpected slap is enough to break a poor mouse's neck. Charles Sebastian had seen it happen. After that, he refused to leave the pantry, and I returned to my doubts. If our own seafaring-adventurer mother couldn't survive, what chance did we have?

Without her we stayed in our crate, more scared than

ever. We sat huddled together, slept curled together, and ate what we could find together. Only I ventured out for water in the dead of night, collecting drips for my brother in the curve of a broken wooden spoon that I gripped between my teeth. There was nothing else that could get us to leave our safe crate now.

Nothing but that word.

ONE DAY WHEN the pantry door opened and Heyu peered into our dark room, a sinister feeling crept in with the fresh sea breeze. It made my fur stand on end. Charles Sebastian froze, then shook. He clamped his mouth onto the bottom slat to chew, which he often did to ease his anxiety. His teeth were admirable, and I was envious of his strong jaw. Gnawing was essential for mice. It got us into places . . . and out of them. A key component to survival. I peered out, looking for cats, but I didn't see any of the monstrous beasts.

"Hey, you!" bellowed the cook from the galley.

"Yes?" said Heyu, turning his pimply face to look at him.

"Grind up some coffee beans. It's going to be a long night."

The boy's eyes widened, but I couldn't guess why.

"Tonight?" he said on a breath.

The cook didn't respond, or at least not loudly enough for us to hear. Heyu came into the pantry. We crouched in the corner of our crate, small as we could be, while the boy hovered over us, his leg a mere tail's length away. The metal coffee scoop crackled as it bit into the goods. It scraped the burlap sack against our fur, and the beans shifted uneasily. Charles Sebastian flattened beneath me and trembled so hard that I thought he was about to bolt. *Fight the urge,* I wanted to tell him, but . . . was it better to run? I was more unsure than ever, and doubts crept and curled in with the fear. My mother's story rang in my ears, and her father's words became her words to me. *It only takes one mouse to believe in you, and that one mouse is me.* I pinched my eyes shut until stillness, and darkness, returned.

But it wouldn't last.

Something Bad

"CLARICE," WHISPERED CHARLES Sebastian sometime later. His trembling had dissipated to a slight but constant shiver. Noises were loud above us; the creaking and groaning of the ship and the boots of the sailors seemed especially heavy.

"Yes, brother," I said. "I'm here."

"The sailors seem more . . . flurrious than usual."

Full of flurry, I thought he meant. *Rushing about.* "Yes."

"The air prickles."

"Does it?" I rose and scraped my paw between his ears to soothe him like Mother used to do. She'd favored him—we all did. As the runt of the litter, he'd always been a bit precious, or at least we treated him that way and he allowed it. Mother once fancied the idea that Charles Sebastian had the gift of future sight—she was very romantic that way, much like with her dreams of seeing the world. I was more pragmatic. And it was clear Charles Sebastian possessed no such gift. After all, he hadn't predicted the giant wave that took our mother away. He hadn't foreseen Special Lady pouncing and grabbing our dear sister Olivia and darting off while the poor thing was still squealing. I'll never forget that sound. Nor the end of it.

If anything, Charles Sebastian possessed more intelligence than the rest of us combined. But he lacked common sense. Perhaps that was what led to his constant state of fear. I'm sure our coddling didn't do him any favors.

Charles Sebastian blinked rapidly. "It's happening," he said.

"What is?"

He didn't answer, but I knew. Cat-paw shadows galloped across the slice of light that came in under the pantry door. Special Lady knew, too—probably more than we did—about the fighting between the two groups of sailors. This ship, full to the gills of boring young oak trees meant to be traded with other nations, was in constant chaos, and half the people blamed the captain for treating them like dirt.

There was a stampede on the ladders—humans were the loudest animals by far. Shouts rang out uncomfortably nearby, and the floorboards shook, making our crate buzz. Then came the zing of metal weapons and a raucous clatter. The dull thuds of fists hitting flesh. We cringed and cringed. The fights had become more frequent in recent days. So had the whippings, ordered by the captain, and the scrape of chains along the decks and inside the human's cage far above us, near the quarterdeck. Everyone muttered. Even the cats were restless.

We were safe in our crate, but the space left by Mother's absence was cold.

"This thing—it's very bad," said Charles Sebastian, growing more agitated. "Mutiny—it means a terrible thing for us. I wish Mother were here. She'd know what to do. Where to run to."

"Shh," I said, stepping tenuously into Mother's protective role, like I imagined she'd want me to do for our littlest bean. "We're completely safe right here. We're not going to run." What else would Mother do right now? It was her presence that had given us comfort, and there was no way for me to replicate that. Inadequacy filled my mind. I was not prepared for any of this. But who could ever be?

More footsteps pounded down the ladders. "Open it!" hollered a woman. "Open this door!" She slammed her fist on the other side of it.

I winced. Lucía. I recognized her voice—she was one of the officers.

We could hear Heyu fumbling with the key in the pantry

padlock. Charles Sebastian panted, the tip of his tongue out. The door swung open, and the handle smacked into the wall; the impact made our teeth rattle. Lucía shoved Heyu aside.

"What's happening?" the boy cried out. Was he pretending not to know?

The woman smacked him hard across the face with the back of her hand. He cried out, and a bloody brown tooth flew into our crate and landed among the coffee beans. Then Lucía stopped short and regarded him as he cowered. "Can you cook?"

"I—I—" said Heyu, bewildered by the question and holding his smarting cheek. His tongue found the gap where his tooth had been. "A little." Then his face paled. "I'm only learning. This is my first . . ." He faltered, overwhelmed.

The woman turned to a group of sailors standing behind her. "Take him up and send him off with the captain. They're going to need a cook when they find land."

"No!" cried the boy. "I don't want to go!" Two of the sailors grabbed Heyu by the arms before he could protest further. "I want to stay with the ship!"

"Don't let the captain hear you say that," someone muttered as they started dragging Heyu away.

The boy came back to life in a panic. "But my half sister! Benjelloun! She's only twelve!" I didn't know Benjelloun, but I understood panic over siblings. Despite my dislike for the boy, I felt a pang of sympathy.

"If we find her, we'll send her with you in the captain's boat," a sailor said.

"Find the girl," Lucía ordered someone we couldn't see. Their footsteps faded.

We shrank down farther as the woman charged back in to survey the shelves.

I'd admired her before. Her long hair was worthy of the finest nest. It hung in coarse brown waves under her hat, with a few loose strands sticking to her face. Sweat shone on her forehead. She leaned over our crate, and I caught a whiff of the rotten stench that spewed out of her mouth with every word. Not much turned my stomach, but her salted-cod rations had been recent, and there was no getting away from it.

She started grabbing crates and tossing them out of the pantry to the remaining sailors. Were we about to be tossed around the galley, too? I sank my claws into the wood and closed my eyes. "Hold on," I whispered. "Dig in."

Charles Sebastian panted, and I worried he would faint.

"That's enough!" shouted a sailor from behind her.

"Leave the rest for us." His eyes were wild and darting. Mother had taught us enough about ship hierarchy to know he shouldn't speak to an officer like that.

We could feel her anger emanating in waves. "Do you wish to be charged with murder on top of treason?" Lucía snarled over her shoulder. "You have to give them provisions."

"Kingsland is only eighty leagues," argued the man.

"In a ship-to-shore boat with a single worn sail that won't withstand the first storm! Do as I say or I'll have you keelhauled." The woman grabbed a half-full crate of salted cod from the bottom shelf, then gathered some moldy, deflated oranges and piled them on top. She tossed it hard at the man. He bobbled it, and a few oranges fell out.

"You're worse than him!" he roared in frustration, and set the crate upright, then shoved it at the sailor behind him.

"Put it in the launch and get out of my sight." Lucía grabbed a small sack of hard biscuits from near us and something else I couldn't see, and passed them back, too. Then her long brown fingers curled over our top slat. She yanked our home across the floor to the door. Charles Sebastian squealed. The sound was lost in the scrape.

"Hold on!" I cried again, not caring who could hear me now. I dug my front claws deeper into the rotting wood.

"Do not run! It's safer in here than under those boot heels!"

Charles Sebastian couldn't speak, but I could feel his heart pounding next to me. We whirled around sickeningly as our crate was handed from one crew person to the next, on and on, beyond the galley and down the ladder-like stairs to the lower deck.

I dared to peek. The light from the fiery torches against the black of night nearly blinded me. The last sailor in the line tossed our crate to the deck, and we skidded and tipped and slammed back down, stopping next to the sack of biscuits. The world spun.

"You're going to regret this," bellowed a man a few feet away. He had ropes twisting around his limbs. His voice was unmistakable—he was the captain, though he looked weak and strange with his hands and ankles tied and his nightshirt on instead of his uniform. His boots were gone, and his toenails curled yellow and black.

While some sailors hung back, perhaps unsure what was happening or whom to side with, a small group lifted the captain over the side of the ship and dropped him. My breath caught, but I heard a heavy clunk instead of a splash. I realized he hadn't fallen far, and soon he struggled and sat up, his head just visible above the railing. It didn't make sense. When my dizziness cleared, I understood it—the launch boat was engaged and suspended above the sea with ropes. The captain had hit his head on the side of it. Blood oozed down his face. "This is treason! You'll be hanged! Mark my words!"

I stared. Lucía arrived, and the captain looked hard at her. "How could you?"

She eyed the man with contempt, but then turned and declared loudly to the rest, "I remain loyal to the captain."

The statement caused another uproar, though I didn't understand why. The captain, disdainful and defiant, waited to see who else was loyal to him. He cast his bloody eye upon each sailor as if memorizing their faces and decisions. Listening intently to their shouts and jeers. Watching the ones who gathered and whispered together with the first officer—the mutinous leader, Mr. Thomas.

A few more declared their loyalty to the captain. They were stripped of their weapons and put in the boat. Still stuck fast between two sailors, Heyu stood miserably on the deck, eyes darting all around in search of his half sister.

"Put him in the launch," Lucía demanded. "Has the girl been found?"

"Who?" asked someone, but Lucía slipped away for a last angry word with Mr. Thomas.

"Benjelloun!" Heyu cried out as the sailors swung him

over the railing. He tried to fight but was no match. After a hard drop, he went silent.

All during this, Charles Sebastian squealed and squirmed, climbing half on top of me and gripping the slat above us with his front claws. "Clarice, we should run."

"No!" I bumped against him, trying to get him to be quiet, but he squealed louder until I finally looked where he was looking. Creeping toward us in the shadow of the ship rail, weaving between crates and ignoring the racket, was Special Lady.

My eyes widened, and I gasped. She'd caught sight of our movements and was staring straight at us.

"Don't move." I slid out from under my brother and tackled him, holding him down, trying to keep him from certain death.

Charles Sebastian may have known the right thing to do. But his fear was stronger than my grip, and he pulled free. He bolted out between the slats before I could stop him and tore a path around sailors' boots, barely keeping from being crushed.

The murderous cat shot after him.

A Small Voice

"CHARLES SEBASTIAN!" I screamed. Then someone picked up my crate and swung it around. "Cha-ah-AH—" My body slipped to one side, and I sank my claws into the wood again. The coffee beans and the bloody tooth and I went airborne, then tipped precariously.

We landed hard in the small boat beside the ship, and my claws wrenched away, leaving the sharp tips of them implanted in the slat. Pain seared through my front paws and stabbed my side. Dazed and overwhelmed, I burrowed under the burlap sack to hide. Blood pinpricked where three of my claws had been ripped to the quick. The pain and impact rattled me hard, and in that moment I forgot about my brother.

Peering out in a daze, I saw Heyu curled up and holding his head, moaning. More items and sailors were being loaded into our little tender. We lurched nauseatingly at each one, and the aching creak of wood against wood was frightful. Like the captain, many of the sailors' and officers' wrists were bound in front of them, tied with ropes. I recognized some by sight or smell. The shocked and miserable looks on their faces told me they knew what was happening . . . and that, perhaps, they realized they were on the wrong side of it.

While the captain continued hollering at the sailors on the ship, calling them mutinous traitors, demanding more food and help, negotiating for more fresh water, my gaze went again to Heyu. This time he seemed to be staring straight at me, which woke me from my daze. He'd stopped shouting for Benjelloun. His eyes were glassy, his lips puffy and downturned, and I think he saw right through me as if I were a spirit. I pushed farther under the burlap, where the torchlight wouldn't betray me.

After some terrible thumps and scrapes, the boat gave a sickening lurch. Shouts rang out. An instant later we were falling.

We hit the water with a jolt, upsetting the sailors and provisions. I'd been nursing my wounds, not holding on to anything, and I flipped out of the crate to the bottom of the boat. Before I could scramble away, a huge wall of water washed over me.

I thought I was dead, washed to the endless sea like my mother. But the water was shallow. Sputtering and choking, I swam for the first time in my life and hoped never to have to do it again. I reached the side of the hull and half clawed my way back up with what remained at the tips of my paws. Then I squeezed through the slats, back to my home under the coffee beans. I could feel my presence of mind fading fast. My teeth chattered from shock, and I shook with cold in the night.

It was then that my heart plunged deep. Charles Sebastian—where was he? Had he survived? Or had he succumbed to the jaws of the brutal Lady? I peered upward and scanned the ship's rail, fruitlessly searching for any sign of my brother, knowing full well he wouldn't be standing on the railing but hoping for it anyway.

A small strip of sea appeared between the vessels, but neither one was moving in earnest yet. It didn't matter. Charles Sebastian was gone, and I was alone. My breath squeezed away until I could force my heart to pump again.

I focused on the captain's voice. "This mutiny will haunt you until the day you die, Mr. Thomas," he bellowed, facing the ship. "I won't rest until I see you all hanging in the gallows!"

Mutiny. There was that word again. And that was what

this complicated mess was called. I'd known it was a fight between two parties, but I still struggled to understand the definition. To those sailors laughing in the ship above us, celebrating their independence from the captain, mutiny meant freedom, and perhaps peace. To the ones with me in this boat, it meant betrayal and shock and fear. It meant being ostracized, abandoned. We were the runts of the litter now, but we'd been cast off instead of coddled.

To me, mutiny meant imminent death. I thought of Charles Sebastian, chased down. If by some miracle I survived whatever this was, I'd have to also survive a broken heart. I'd never see him again. The truth set me on fire— every follicle of fur ached and burned. What was there to live for now?

I heard a young human voice crying far away. Heyu's half sister? I couldn't bear it. As our boatful of rejects drifted under a single torn sail, and the strip of sea began to grow between us, a faint, familiar squeak came from the ship. "Clarice!"

My heart clutched, and I couldn't draw a breath. Had shock or delusion set in? Was his voice in my head part of my new nightmare?

I turned my ears, listening for a sound anyone else would scarcely notice, and I heard it again. "Clarice!"

I leaned between the slats, straining my eyes, but I couldn't see him. "Charles Sebastian!" I squeaked in the din.

"Come back," he said through sobs. "Come back!"

It broke me. I looked at the rough waves. The widening distance between my boat and his ship. There was no way I could swim it. No way I could climb the sheer, slimy side of the ship even if I made it that far without drowning. I was too afraid to try. "I can't."

"I'll come with you," Charles Sebastian cried.

"Stay where you are!" I screamed before it was too late—if my impulsive brother jumped now, he'd never survive. "I'll find you," I promised. "I'll find you, Charles Sebastian. Use your mind. Stay alive!" Then, as a desperate echo of my mother, I added, "It only takes one mouse to believe in you! And that one mouse is me!"

Perhaps it would give him the courage I lacked. But how I worried that my brother was doomed.

Just then the captain shouted again, his voice wretched and desperate, his wrists freed from the ropes and his fist pounding air. The boat shifted, and he slammed his foot into my crate. I hit my head. Coffee beans spilled from the sack and smothered me, and everything went dark.

Misery

"CLARICE," CHARLES SEBASTIAN called again. But this time his sister didn't answer. Devastated, he let his body slump to the deck. His life had been spared, saved from the orange ogre, Special Lady, by a sailor who'd scooped her up and carried her off, foiling her plans. But what was there to live for now? Clarice was gone. There was no way his sister could survive in such a small boat with all those humans. As far as Charles Sebastian was concerned, humans were the worst enemies—even to each other.

Two such enemies whispered nearby. "They don't have enough water to last a week," said one.

"The sea was nearly breaching the gunwales as it was," said the other. "They couldn't take one more person, let alone the dozen who wanted to stand with that tyrant. We've locked the worst of them in the brig." She hesitated, then added, "That launch is sure to sink in the first storm."

"I fear for it. But . . ."

Footsteps approached, and the two sailors turned. A harried officer yanked a young sailor along with him. "It's too late," he snarled, ignoring the girl's sobs. He turned to the two. "I finally found her—skulking in the shadows around Mr. Thomas. Listening in. I'm afraid she heard way too much, and Thomas is furious. Help me with her, will you?" The group of them moved away together, leaving Charles Sebastian alone.

"Clarice," he said again, this time in a mournful whisper. He should have jumped after her despite her cries against it. He'd be no worse off if he'd done it and drowned.

She'd said she'd find him. And though Charles Sebastian was a runt, he was smart. Smart enough to know better. Everything about the sea was evil—the waves, the sailors, the cats—and he'd probably never see his sister again. His eyes glistened. Clarice was all he had left. Without her he felt lost.

He was also physically lost. Special Lady had chased him to an unfamiliar part of the ship, and despite Charles Sebastian's intelligence, he was terrible with directions and had no idea how to find the pantry again. Personal flaws like this had prompted his more commonsensical siblings and mother to treat him like a baby. And he had to admit he hadn't stopped them, because why would he? It was kind of nice to be waited on. But now he wished he'd paid more attention to the layout of the ship rather than always following someone else around.

He shivered against the salty wind, which forced tufts of his fur to pull against the grain in an uncomfortable way. Where was he? He'd run hard and fast, jumping up multiple flights of steps and avoiding boots like an acrobat. Nothing looked familiar out here in this wide-open space—he could have been dropped from the stars. It made Charles Sebastian dizzy and queasy to look up at them while the ship pitched and rolled. He had to find his pantry, but after everything that had happened, the task overwhelmed him.

"She believes in me," he whispered, remembering, and felt a surge of fortitude from it. But the words puzzled him, too, because his family hadn't exactly expressed their belief in him before. They'd doubted his instincts to run time and time again. They'd talked openly about his intense fears, as if having them made one weaker. Charles Sebastian would argue that his fears made him stronger. Physically, anyway, from running so much. He sighed, for there was no one left to debate with. Maybe

Clarice really had meant the words she'd shouted.

But how was his dear sister faring? Could she possibly survive her situation, with sailors and seawater everywhere? He doubted it, and the doubt made him feel raw inside. *I believe in you, too,* he thought, despite everything. And even if Clarice hadn't fully meant it, perhaps she'd wanted to believe it, which was almost as good. Both receiving and giving the words gave Charles Sebastian courage to keep going.

After shivering for a while, he skittered toward a tall cage that had long chains clunking against the solid back wall with every roll of the ship. There was a girl sitting inside it with her knees drawn up and head down. It was the young sailor he'd seen earlier, being yanked by the officer. Charles Sebastian didn't know her, which meant she probably worked in another part of the ship.

The girl's wrists were tied with rope, and her ankles had chains attached to them, which seemed especially harsh and mean-spirited since she was already imprisoned on the exposed upper deck. But Charles Sebastian had seen these sailors intentionally hurting each other before, so he wasn't terribly surprised. Perhaps they'd shackled her because she was like Charles Sebastian—especially good at gnawing, or small enough to squeeze through the wooden bars—and the officers feared her escape. He eyed the uneven spacing between the bars. This cage was built for full-grown sailors, not children.

The girl's torso began to shake silently. She didn't notice him.

Charles Sebastian crept along the outside of the cage, trying to breathe properly as fear pulsed in his chest. He went around the solid back wall and discovered a small enclosed coop centered on the other side. It had an open arched doorway and a ramp leading up to it. Charles Sebastian could just see a layer of stale straw poking out, which looked warm. Darting up the ramp, Charles Sebastian peered inside. Three large balls of feathers sat there—and their scent told him they were alive. He'd never seen anything like them before and tried to comprehend what he was looking at. Were these the notorious chickens Mother had warned them about?

Charles Sebastian had heard the cook talk to Heyu about fetching eggs from Mabel, one of the ship's chickens. And Mother had told the young mice that the fowl roamed freely, sometimes going belowdecks when the rain blew sideways into their coop. "They'll peck your eyes out," Mother warned them. "Steer clear when they're wandering. It's not beyond a chicken's good conscience to eat a bothersome mouse." Charles Sebastian hadn't run into any of them before, which only served to increase his anxiety now that he'd found their lair.

Panic struck hard, and Charles Sebastian felt the overwhelming urge to bolt again. Would he ever be safe? He had escaped the dreaded cat, only to find himself about to be blinded or eaten by a chicken. When would this night of horror end?

He fled down the ramp and across the deck, swerving in a most reckless manner toward the bow, until he saw a staircase. He skidded to a stop at the top of it, remembering that he'd come up ladders on his earlier flight from Special Lady. Which meant down was the right way to go. He navigated his way, hopping and resting to help with his shaking. One step at a time, focusing on getting to the bottom.

But when he reached the deck below and scooted around the base of the ladder, nothing looked familiar. Where was the galley? Where was his pantry? All he wanted was to be someplace familiar. Someplace that felt like home.

A barely audible footfall made Charles Sebastian turn his head sharply. Another blasted orange cat—Marigold this time! His pounding heart threatened to split his chest open. He spied a coil of thick rope under the steps and dove inside, then jammed his body alongside the bottom coil. Had Marigold seen him?

He was frighteningly lost. Thirsty and hungry. Faint from exhaustion. Broken with grief. And now this. His soul dove deep into the shadows as he imagined Marigold's yellow eyes coming for him.

Charles Sebastian trembled against the rough rope fibers. The runt of the litter, possibly the only survivor of his entire family, closed his eyes and waited for the jaws of death to take him.

On the Open Sea

I AWOKE TO a terrible odor and discovered Heyu's rotten tooth beneath my head. After leaping away from its rankness, I discovered my fur was sticky and coated with brown slime. At first I thought it was from the tooth, but a sniff told me it was from the soupy coffee beans. As I found my bearings and tried to clean my fur, my injured front claws thudded dully with my heartbeat.

The captain was talking quietly with Lucía and a man called Tembe near the center of the boat. Others were asleep, leaning on crates or lying on the floor of the boat with their heads propped on the gunwales. It was still dark, but the palest hue of pink tipped the edge of the sky where it met the sea.

The ship was gone.

Its lack of existence shook me. And the sea . . . was everywhere. It was calm, yet as we rolled through the low, wide waves, small amounts of water spilled in. The launch was overladen. One big wave and I'd be swept away again.

I had to find a higher, drier hiding spot before daylight screamed in. Forcing my worries aside, I glanced around, sizing up my options, and spied the point of the bow. There was a broad triangular piece of wood, like a flat roof, that covered the open storage space underneath. Some of the sacks and crates from the pantry had already been shoved into the space—to keep them dry, I assumed. Their familiarity in appearance and scent was comforting . . . although to my great unease I also picked up the odor of a wet animal. Perhaps it was just the soaked sailors sitting in the dank water at the bottom of the boat. There wasn't enough room on the benches for everyone.

I plotted my journey, realizing there was no getting around the various sailors who were sprawled every which way. As the sky's color spread and my chances of being discovered grew, I scurried around an ankle, jumped over a face and an arm, and darted into the space behind the sack of hard biscuits and another one of flour. The space was wonderfully dark and naturally protected from sea spray. I hoped to survive an hour, a day . . . however long it would take to locate Charles Sebastian and get back to him. That he was alive cheered me significantly, though I hadn't yet begun to figure out how to find him. My good cheer was fleeting, though, and it dissipated completely when I remembered Charles Sebastian's nature. He would be frightened without me. And his fear led to things like bolting from our crate when Special Lady came near. If it hadn't been for that impulsive move, we'd be together. I closed my eyes, pained, and tried not to think about how his urges to run were probably going to be the end of him.

My imagination began to get the better of me, and frightening images crowded my thoughts. My eyes flew open. Special Lady and Marigold and the other ship animals would be skulking about. He'd know enough to find a small space that those larger beasts couldn't get to, but would he be cold and lonely without me? Would he be able to find water and food? He could gnaw wood for hours, and figure out what words meant, and calculate the length of time it would take a mouse to run from one end of the pantry to the other. But did he know enough to look for water when he got thirsty, or had I become his crutch when it came to necessities?

Surely he'd gone back to the pantry once the deck was clear, but our crate was here with me, so he'd need to build a new nest. Did he have any idea how to do that? And what if he hadn't been able to find his way there? I didn't think he'd ever been to the quarterdeck before—I'd only been there once myself—but he must have been there when he shouted to me or I wouldn't have heard him so well.

To calm my worries, I closed my eyes and pictured him back in the pantry, finding a new home among the potatoes and grain, nibbling on a hard crust of a bread roll or a bitter slice of orange peel, taking a cautious drink from the galley where the cleaned stew pots hung and dripped water onto the floorboards.

Slowly, my beating heart softened until I didn't hear the thudding in my ears anymore. I cleaned my fur, then tucked my nose under my paws and drifted off to sleep. I dreamed of Mother and Olivia and Charles Sebastian and the rest of us all curled up comfortably in a bed of straw. Nowhere near water.

When I opened my eyes, the dream shattered.

I was alone and cold. And staring at me from the center of the launch was a sodden, miserable orange lump of fur. My heartbeat exploded in my ears again. Special Lady was here. In this little boat. Somehow in the mayhem she had been cast out of the ship, tossed down to her master. With eleven filthy sailors and me.

Instinct begged me to jump out of the boat. To take a

chance on the water turning to glass so I could run forever. But I willed myself to hold steady.

Special Lady's sharp eye was on me. She knew I was here—that was the worst part of it. She'd seen me before I'd detected her, and I chastised myself for it. I knew I'd smelled something, but I never thought it could be her. How regrettable that I'd been fooled into believing my biggest enemy here was the flat of a sailor's boot or the slow spill of a waterfall over the gunwale. Cats were the ultimate enemy.

Ah, but at least it meant Charles Sebastian was safe from this marmalade scoundrel. Because I was more capable of keeping my head than Charles Sebastian was—especially around a cat—our chances of reuniting increased slightly. But in these close quarters, with limited food . . . maybe I was being a bit too generous in my odds. How long before the cat was the first one knocked off the captain's list of rations? The only good cat was a fed cat. And even then, still not good at all.

Special Lady looked down her nose at me with disdain. Then, instead of coming at me, she turned her face and started licking her matted, wet fur, which unsettled me more than if she'd kept staring. Was it a ploy? A trick? Probably. This was a game I didn't want to play.

When my head cleared and I could think like a proper intelligent mouse again, I lifted my nose and glared at the cat, baring my teeth. I wouldn't go down without a fight.

She noticed, though she pretended not to.

I moved out of sight, deeper inside the crate, where she probably wouldn't be able to reach. I'd sleep with one eye open.

"I'LL NEVER FORGIVE them," Heyu muttered to no one, though his voice in my general vicinity woke me with a start. "Never."

Lucía overheard, too. "They tried," she said.

"Hardly," Heyu said bitterly.

Lucía's eyes shifted. "I . . . thought I saw her briefly, but then she ran. We're too full anyway."

Heyu didn't answer.

At first I wasn't sure what they were talking about. But then I remembered. There was no child on this boat besides him. His half sister, Benjelloun, hadn't been delivered to the launch. I felt a fresh pang of empathy for the apprentice cook, but it didn't last. I had no energy for his sorrow on top of my own.

The humans were loud, then lethargic under the sun. They didn't eat, and only drank a little from their stores.

I wasn't sure where my sustenance would come from. I could find crumbs easily enough in the crates, but fresh water would be hard to come by since the sailors' supply was secured. There was always something to worry about.

When night fell, a streak of lightning and a crack of thunder made the sailors groan. Soon we were rocking from side to side. Waves breached the gunwales, splashing in. Giant drops of rain bigger than my nose struck the ragged, thirsty sail and soaked in. The sailors tripped and slipped as they scurried to keep the boat afloat, scooping out the seawater with one hand and collecting as much of the rain as they could with the other.

Special Lady, who'd been almost dry before the downpour began, bolted to the stern for cover under the lip of the transom. She melted into a ball, elbows poking upward, and peeked out at the clouds. The menacing glow of her yellow eyes looked even more sinister with the backdrop of forked lightning in a mottled sky.

The rain called. I eased out of my spot and crept along the crate slat, never taking my eyes off Special Lady, until raindrops struck the point of my nose. I lapped them up as the wretched ginger mop tensed, unable to resist a moving mouse despite the weather. Every hour of my survival counted as a win against the beast, but she was no doubt

growing hungry by now, and I doubted the sailors would be catering to her.

So focused was I on the cat that I neglected to notice Heyu sliding farther and farther into the storage space under the point of the bow, trying to find shelter from the torrent. As Special Lady raised her back end and shifted side to side, ready to bolt straight at me, I slipped inside the crate. When I turned to look through the slat to see if she was coming, I found myself face-to-face with Heyu. His cheek bulged and he looked a mess.

He lunged for me.

With a squeal, I dove out of sight, scrambling into a fold of burlap. Not realizing it was the sack of flour, I burrowed into it. The powder filled my nostrils and coated my teeth. Too late I realized that the only escape was certain suffocation. My enemies were increasing, and my minutes remaining in this world were numbered.

Choking and coughing, emitting tiny clouds into the air, I fought my way out of the sack and beelined deeper into the point of the bow. Heyu's fingers swiped clumsily this way and that. He connected with my backside, sending me sliding. With a frantic leap, I reached the crate's wood slats, and near one corner I discovered a rather large knothole. I pressed my heaving sides into it. It was a tight fit, but safe from both enemies, and I swore I'd never move again if only I could survive Heyu's deadly swinging appendages.

He gave up.

I remained still for a long time. A thin dough formed from the flour that had gotten inside my mouth, and I couldn't seem to swallow it. Misery set in. The only thing holding me steady was the memory of my brother's voice. I said I'd find him. He said he'd find me.

One of us had to be right.

Preventive Measures

I THOUGHT ABOUT loss, perhaps more than a young mouse should. All the time it was on my mind. Waking up to find my siblings still and cold in the nest, or hearing their screams as the cat bites down, then the silence. My mother was there one moment, teaching us about the world, saying lovely things to me. Then gone in a blink.

There were so many unspoken questions that followed. Did she suffer? Did any of them? In my sister Olivia's last instant, did she ever wonder about us—wonder why we didn't help her? I knew it wasn't my fault, but with so much time to think, the guilt was heavy on my heart. Did she still blame me in some spirit-like afterlife?

"Mother," I whispered from the knothole in the dead of night, "if you can hear me, tell Charles Sebastian I am still alive. And we will find each other. Tell him I really do believe in him . . . like you believed in me. Like your father believed in you." I cringed, fighting off doubt. Whether my message reached her or not, sending it over the waves eased my troubled mind.

I wished we hadn't coddled Charles Sebastian quite so much. I wished I were a simpler mouse, able to forget the ones who died, like most mice naturally do when absence grows long. That would be easier. Though it would give me less to live for.

Then my eyes flew open. *What if Charles Sebastian forgets me?*

After a moment of panic, I returned to my senses. He wouldn't forget me. And I wouldn't forget him. Not ever.

ONE OR TWO of the sailors were always awake, keeping watch, turning the pitiful torn sail to catch the wind. There was a single oar as well, but it didn't seem to help much, and the captain barked when the boat wasn't going exactly the way he wanted. Sometimes Tembe worked on the sail, trying to fix the rips. "Tie the loose pieces together," Lucía suggested. "At least it'll keep the rest from tearing more." They had no tools to do anything else. I eyed the tatters, wishing for a piece to add to my nest.

"When are we going to eat something?" Heyu whined. He'd been ordered by Lucía to stop whining about his sister, so he'd turned to the next thing on his mind.

Apparently he'd abandoned all decorum, for he shouldn't be speaking at all in such company without being spoken to first.

The captain, Lucía, and Tembe all turned sharply and silenced him with a look. Heyu shrank back, abashed. I could hear his innards churning from where I sat. He was already thin and would no doubt grow thinner before this was over. He held his hand to his cheek, which was still swollen and getting worse.

The captain turned back to look over the sea. He consulted an instrument that seemed to give him hints about where land was. "We're off course!" he barked, startling everyone. He did something with the sail and yelled some unsavory words at the crew.

Lucía didn't flinch. "How far have we traveled, Captain?"

The man squinted into the sun. "Five leagues. Seven at most. A snail's pace." I didn't understand distance like Charles Sebastian did, but I'd heard a sailor on the ship say Kingsland was eighty leagues away, and that seemed like a much higher number. At this point I didn't ever expect to see land. There was only water. We were hardly moving, or so it seemed from my limited view.

"We're going to need to eat something today," Lucía said to him in a low voice.

After a time, the captain relented. "Kitchen boy," he barked. "Where's the list of rations?"

"I—I—don't have a list."

The captain stared. "Have you learned nothing in your time as an apprentice?"

"There's no pencil—"

"Find a different way," shouted the captain. "What do we have? Keep the list in your mind."

Heyu struggled to take account of the food, saying things aloud as he saw them. I shrank back inside my knothole as he assessed my crate. Finally he turned to the barrel and lifted the lid. "Brined beef. More brine than beef."

The captain blew out an annoyed breath. "Leave that for now. Pass out a square-inch ration of salted cod to each of us," he told Heyu. "That's it."

The kitchen boy returned to the crate he used as a seat and reached inside. He unwrapped a fillet and broke off a piece. The smell turned my stomach.

"Smaller," the captain ordered. "Half that size." He muttered under his breath, "Doesn't know an inch from a mile."

Heyu, hands trembling, broke the piece in two and carefully handed them both to Lucía, who passed them with the utmost care down to the opposite end of the boat.

Special Lady jumped to attention the moment the salted

cod came out. Her meows pierced the air as she hopped from one sailor to a bench, to another sailor to the deck, making her way to Heyu, who'd often fed her scraps in the kitchen. "Do I give her some?"

The crew erupted in dissent.

"Okay, okay," said Heyu. He swiped at the sweat in his eyes and winced when he bumped his swollen cheek. "Get away," he said, swatting at Special Lady in frustration. "There's none for you." She tried again, and Heyu picked her up and set her down farther away. Special Lady moved to the captain, chittering at him as he took his bite-size piece, and tried to push her nose into his hand. He swore and shoved her aside, then blocked her with his arm when she persisted.

I took a bit of sick pleasure in watching the rusty old feline get denied. That is, until she glanced *my* way.

My breath caught. Special Lady was hungry, and no one was feeding her. That meant I was her number-one meal option unless I could find something else for her. So that night, when most of the sailors nearest me were asleep and Special Lady stopped her pitiful mewing and settled into a lap at the stern, I began to do a little inventory of my own.

There was the sack of hard biscuits. I dragged one back to my crate and enjoyed a quick nibble. But I didn't think the cat was desperate enough to gnaw on rock-hard tack when there was a juicy mouse to be had. That left the coffee, the sack of flour, the small crate of salted cod, and the brined beef. I put my ear to the barrel, listening to the sloshing inside as we rode the waves. It sounded heavy. If Charles Sebastian were here, he'd talk endlessly about how the barrel would weigh our boat down less if they emptied some of the brine. Heyu, being the kitchen boy, should be the one to come up with that idea, but I had no confidence in his mind at all.

I wasn't about to go fishing for beef for the cat, anyway—they'd find me pickled at the bottom on their last day of rations. So salted cod it was. Unfortunately, that crate was currently beneath Heyu's putrid, rotting boots. And the boy's revolting feet were inside the boots. He was sleeping at the moment with an arm thrown over his eyes, so there was that.

The cat's eyes drooped, and she rested her chin on her paws for a nap. I had to go in. I eased between the slats of my crate and moved stealthily around the other supplies that were jammed into the point of the bow. The bottom corner of the crate below Heyu's stacked boots had a space the size of the broken spoon I'd used to transport water. Big enough for me to squirm into.

Once I was inside, my nose stung from the odor of dried fish. I nibbled open the paper it was wrapped in, careful to keep the hole as small as possible so Heyu might not notice it—rule one of pantry living, according to our mother. Then I gnawed off a chunk of the stuff and dragged it out.

Heyu shifted and clunked his boots above my head, and I nearly dropped the salted cod in fright. But then he settled and I continued out, peering between the slats. The smell of the fillet was nauseating, and I knew I'd taste it on my teeth and tongue for quite some time. It reminded me of the sea I hated so much. What could my mother have possibly loved about it? I couldn't understand. But I'd never seen an alternative—maybe land was even worse. But did land ever swell and slap mothers away?

I pushed the hunk of fish out through the slat until I heard its soft landing on the bottom of the boat, and then I went to collect it. I dragged it to my crate and hid it where Special Lady couldn't reach, under the corner of the flour sack. Then I went back for more.

By morning I had enough pieces to open a shop. I went back to close up the package as best I could. By the time the crew members were stirring, I was ready for a nap. But before I went to sleep, I slid a small hunk of the fish outside of my crate, hidden from the sailors but not from Special Lady. Before I drifted off, she was in my space, sniffing around.

"Leave me alone and I'll feed you," I said to her, my voice shaking even though I was safe. I don't know if she understood. But I was too tired to care.

WHEN I AWOKE, the piece of fish was gone and Special Lady was nowhere to be seen.

Learning Tolerance

THE CAT'S DISAPPEARANCE was probable cause for panicking.

Either she'd gone overboard—which would be fine by me, but I doubted that was the case—or she was hiding somewhere new. Mother told us that cats were mystically fluid. Like mice, they could ease and squeeze into places you'd never suspect. Before moving from my knothole, I looked in all directions, even behind me into the darkest point of the bow.

Nothing.

I poked my head out farther, and the swish of a tail overhead caught my eye. Special Lady was flattened above me, on top of my crate, staring down at me through the space between the slats. I caught my breath as she reached a mud-drenched paw down as far as she could, curling and uncurling those padded toes. She batted in my direction.

Once I could tell how far she could reach and realized it was not as far as me, I eased out of my spot and slid down to my stash. I wanted her to see me give her food. I'm not sure why—maybe it was because feeding someone felt powerful. Perhaps, with my logic, the fed became beholden to the provider. That was my hope, anyway. There was only one way I would succeed with this plan, and that was to be more tenacious than I'd ever been. I had to show Special Lady who was in charge.

I took the smallest piece of fish and waved it like a flag so she could see it. An offering . . . or a trick. The texture aggravated my tongue, but this was my life now. Once I climbed to the top of my crate, I shoved it between the slats so she could get it. Then I darted out of reach. "If you eat me," I declared, "you'll feel full for half a day. But if you keep me around? There's a lot more where this came from. I'll make sure you stay alive."

Special Lady touched her nose daintily to the fish, then licked it. Then she took it between her pointy teeth. She was missing a few, like Heyu, but she had enough to tackle a mouse. I thought of Olivia and cringed. The cat chewed and swallowed the fish down, then sniffed the wooden crate for more.

I brought a second piece. She swiped at it, cuffing me

in the face, and I spat it at her. "I am your provider," I said in a stern voice. "I'm your . . . your mother." I wrinkled my nose at the image, but pushed forward. "You need me more than you need anyone on this boat. They won't feed you, but I will. If I die, you die."

She didn't respond. Had I made a mistake? I didn't know if she understood what I was saying—we mice had never tried speaking to a cat before. But we didn't need words to communicate. I feigned toughness because it was the only option I had. I could not survive the sea *and* two enemies in such a small space. There was no easy way to get Heyu to stand down. So here we were.

After that, Special Lady didn't leave my space except to stretch her legs or beg sailors for a nibble of the brined beef that the captain allowed them to eat that day. But I kept my stash safe. And she didn't come after me. Yet.

The doubts crept in. Had I been too arrogant? Had I angered her? Perhaps she was waiting to give me a false sense of confidence before she put me in my place. My mother's words tried and failed to soothe me to sleep. *It only takes one mouse . . .*

Hanging On

CHARLES SEBASTIAN DIDN'T die by cat.

He gnawed a shallow pit into the curl of thick rope and stayed flattened inside it while the creaks of the ship played an endless song in his head. But then someone came and took the coil and nearly squashed him. He was homeless again, and ran blindly to a dark corner under the stairs.

Time crawled by, but Charles Sebastian didn't pay attention. There had been days and nights since Clarice was tossed into the launch. He was starving, but nothing sounded good to eat except the salt on his nose.

He spent a day dozing and startling awake and dozing again, crouched in his filthy corner. He feared he'd freeze and become a statue if he remained motionless for much longer. Or perhaps he'd turn into a spirit to haunt the underside of the ladders. Enemies beware.

It was only a dream to be that brave. Instead, his mind

was filled with numbers. How many ladders had he come up when Special Lady first chased him? How many heartbeats would it take him to run the length of this deck? How far, how much? He could calculate distance but had no sense of direction. If only Clarice were here to shoulder half this burden of finding their way home. She'd know in an instant. How many heartbeats away was she right now?

The atmosphere was stark out here. Charles Sebastian missed the clink of dishes. The soothing ripple of coffee beans shifting with the roll of the sea. The syrupy scent of rotting citrus. But he couldn't bear the thought of endlessly searching for the pantry only to find it empty of love.

As he stayed very still, two sailors met at the bottom of the ladder and spoke in whispers.

"They're going to try to find us."

"Who?"

"You know who. From the launch." He looked over his shoulder uneasily.

"Oh." A pause. "When?"

"After we drop off the remaining loyalists and they lose you-know-who and the rest."

"You-know-who?"

The smart one sighed and gave up the pretense of

vagueness. "The captain, you idiot. And his supporters."

"Oh. So we'll meet them at the island?"

"Shh. Don't breathe another word." They parted, acting as if they hadn't spoken at all.

Charles Sebastian cocked his head quizzically. The conversation was cryptic, yet a few of the phrases echoed in his mind, seeming very important. Who could they be talking about? Charles Sebastian thought it had been a simple, logical split—mutiny supporters on the ship, captain supporters on the launch. But what it sounded like now was that there were people on this ship who wanted to be with the captain. And people on Clarice's boat who wanted to be with the ship. And once the mutineers got rid of the captain supporters, they were going to try to reunite with the ones from the captain's launch on some island.

So if Clarice was smart enough to stay alive and pay attention . . . maybe there really was a chance she could end up in the same place as Charles Sebastian.

It seemed terribly complicated, and the chances of complicated things coming together properly were small. But according to his calculations, the probability of seeing Clarice again had just gone from zero to something greater than zero. And that was an excellent reason not to give up. With heavy limbs and aching joints from being still for so long, Charles Sebastian wearily restarted his existence and dragged himself up to the top deck.

The sun bit down on his back, warming him, reviving him. He hadn't spent much of his life in daylight and preferred darkness because it was friendlier. But he quite enjoyed wearing the heat like a cloak for a moment. He trudged to the area where Special Lady had chased him. A tiny part of him was still hoping the cat would show up and unexpectedly pounce and end his misery. But then the fading memory of Olivia came to mind. That wouldn't be a quick or satisfactory solution. He'd rather go back to haunting the stairwell. Besides, what if there was something to what the sailors had whispered?

Avoiding boots, he made his way up to the quarter-deck. The aging wood of the mizzenmast beckoned to him like a grandfather. Charles Sebastian answered the call and climbed the mast far enough to be able to see over the ship's railing. Anything too far away would be a blur, but there were only waves to be blurry. He moved around the mast, spending a moment scouring each direction.

There was nothing.

The melancholy feeling he'd been having settled deep inside him like a rattling cough. Did he dare hope? As

Charles Sebastian rested, suspended from the mast, looking out over the sea, an image of his mother came to mind. And the last words that she'd ever said to him before she'd been swept away rang in his ears. He'd kept the words close, not even telling Clarice, for it had been too hard. "Stay together, little bean," she'd said. "In sight and mind. Even after I'm gone." She'd paused as they'd ventured out. "I want to tell you a story about my father—" Then came the wave.

Charles Sebastian's eyes watered, perhaps from the wind or glare. Or from the reminder. He and Clarice couldn't be together in sight right now. But Mother had provided an alternative. *In mind.* It would have to do. He rested his head against the mast, feeling strength and power and safety emanating from it. It had to be true.

AFTER A WHILE, he descended to the deck, hunger and thirst blooming. The pantry was becoming a fuzzy memory, as if it no longer existed without Clarice. It was time to find a new home.

When he skittered around the corner of the human's cage, the girl was still inside, ankles shackled and wrists bound, as before. She was sitting in almost the same position as when he'd seen her days ago. The remaining loose chains clapped against the wooden bars, reminding

Charles Sebastian of sounds from the galley, which was almost comforting despite the terror the kitchen boy had instilled. There was a bowl at the young sailor's side with something in it that smelled negatively interesting. But next to it was half of a hard biscuit and a tin cup.

A wave of nausea and hunger passed through Charles Sebastian, and with a renewed burst of energy, he darted inside the pen and snuck up behind the prisoner, then peered up at her.

Her eyes were closed.

Charles Sebastian tried to think of what Clarice might do. She was the most sensible mouse he knew. She was always imagining innovative things, like using the broken spoon to carry water to him when he was too afraid to leave the pantry. He studied the chains. Clarice would notice them and point out that their tautness meant the girl couldn't go far. And with her wrists tied with rope in front of her . . . He closed his eyes, trying to see things like Clarice did. If the biscuit somehow moved out of the girl's reach, he determined, there was nothing she could do except roar at the mouse who'd moved it there.

Roaring was bad, but it wasn't lethal.

Charles Sebastian calculated the distance he had to go to get out of reach, and the time it would take to get that far. With shaking limbs, the mouse crept forward, his mouth watering, until he made it to his target. Ever so slowly, he reached for the tack, hooked a claw on one of the uneven nubs, and pulled. It scraped off the edge of the plate and thunked to the deck. Charles Sebastian froze. But the prisoner didn't open her eyes.

The mouse re-hooked his claw and inched backward, pulling the biscuit. He paused to take a quick nibble in case he had to abandon the plan. After that, he continued dragging it over to the leeward side of the cage and pressed himself into the corner, his back to the solid wall. He left the biscuit there and skittered over to the tin cup. Sniffing it, he could tell it wasn't water. It smelled sour, like the sailors' sweat at night. Charles Sebastian sat up on his haunches and stretched, reaching a paw to the top of the cup. He knocked it over, making a clatter that had the girl stirring awake. Quickly, Charles Sebastian sipped some of the liquid before it soaked into the deck. Then he darted back to the corner.

"Hey!" said the girl, sitting up and turning to watch the rodent escape. "What do you think you're doing?" She quickly set the cup upright in hopes of saving some of the contents. "Where's the rest of my biscuit?"

The drink had tasted like liquid dirt, and it made Charles Sebastian feel woozy. But it was something. He sat,

eyes crossed, with the half biscuit propped in front of him between his paws, and nibbled away. He forgot about the prisoner, forgot his worries, and only thought about his appetite, which had come roaring back.

The girl turned her body and watched in frustration as the mouse ate her rations. She lunged at the offender but didn't get far. "You'll end up in jail like me if you keep that up! And thanks a lot for dousing the deck boards with my grog, you little beast." She wrinkled her nose in disgust and moved away from the spill. "My trousers are soaked."

Charles Sebastian made a little humming noise as he ate, his lids half closed, his ears focused only on the scrape of his teeth against the tack. He didn't notice the chicken high-stepping along the deck, looking for someone to feed her.

When boots pounded the deck, the chicken fluttered and disappeared around the corner. Charles Sebastian's eyes flew open at the sound, and then he froze. One of the sailors he'd seen earlier stopped in front of the cage to collect the dishes from the prisoner. When he stooped down, he whispered to her. "We're going to make a stop to let off all the loyalists who couldn't fit in the captain's boat."

The girl looked up sharply. "Including me?"

"No, of course not," said the man. "You know too much, and Mr. Thomas is furious about it. You won't be getting any favors from him, I can assure you."

"I don't know anything," the girl cried out. "I wasn't listening to his silly plans. I was . . . hiding. Because I was *scared*." She sounded like she was lying.

The man scoffed. "You're staying with us all the way to . . . the place."

"But my brother!" She made a hacking noise in her throat, then spat at him, hitting his boot. "You're all monsters!"

"Hey!" The man kicked the bars, annoyed, then seemed to take pity on the girl. He wiped the boot on the back of his other leg, then took a step back. "Chances are, if he survives a watery grave, he'll go straight back to the mainland with the captain to testify against us. And you're definitely not going there to help them." He paused. "We'll be very far away by then."

Listening In

I SHOULD HAVE been paying more attention to the conversations.

It's not that mice don't understand what humans are saying. It's just that humans are always talking, and it becomes monotonous and repetitive and squawkish, like a seagull circling a sailor who has a bit of food in his hand. Back in the pantry, Charles Sebastian and I heard the sailors chatter all the time and mostly ignored them. But when the word *mutiny* was said in whispers, it stood out. That was when we listened.

Charles Sebastian and I had enjoyed debating the definition. We'd argued over its exact meaning, and I daresay he still believes it to be something different than I do today because of our circumstances surrounding it. To him it might mean overthrowing the captain. To me, keeping the captain around and suffering for it. But to both of us, mutiny meant separation that might never end.

"Tell me about your sister," Lucía asked Heyu one night. The two were assigned the late watch.

"Half sister," Heyu said, then added miserably, "I'm responsible for her."

"Why you? What about her parents?"

"They're both officers on other ships. Our mother's ship is lost at sea. Benjelloun's father—my stepfather—was due in port a week before the *Carlotta* set sail."

"But it didn't show up?"

"That's right." The boy shook his head, as if regretting every move he'd made from that point on. "Her father intended to return home and remain with her so I could go on my first post. But his ship didn't arrive in time. I didn't know if it was lost at sea like our mother's, or just delayed. I couldn't leave Benjelloun home alone, so I brought her with me. She wanted to be a sailor," Heyu assured Lucía. "And she's been earning her keep swabbing the decks." His eyes darted guiltily to the sleeping captain. "But now—" Heyu choked up and didn't continue. He held his hand to his swollen red cheek. "Hurts to talk," he said gruffly, and turned away. "I don't feel well."

"I hope you all reunite one day soon." Lucía's face clouded, as if she didn't believe it would happen. "Let's have a look at your mouth when morning comes."

* * *

THE DAYS PASSED. Heyu, in pain, became insufferable in his whining. Of course I felt sorry for him, for his situation was much like mine. But there comes a point when no amount of empathy can overcome incessant moans. I blamed him for being the seagull that caused me to shut everyone out when I should have been paying attention. I blamed the titian fuzzball, too, for keeping me extremely occupied for a couple of days. I felt like I was running my own galley while dodging giant sledgehammers falling from the sky. Attempting to accomplish a difficult task while always looking up and darting about to avoid death was no lark.

Watching Heyu, I determined that pain changes a human in a different way than it changes a mouse. Mice focus all their energy on healing. Heyu focused all his on annoying everyone. Half the time he just made noise but said no words—no wonder I didn't pay attention. Granted, his sunburned face was turning redder by the day and beginning to blister and crack and peel. But his cheek had continued to swell and was now twice its size. His health was getting worse, not better. That was cause for alarm. Tembe fixed him a poultice out of flour, precious water, and a piece of his shirt to help ease Heyu's pain and draw out the infection. But it didn't seem to be working.

Once Heyu had the compress shoved into his mouth,

and the fur-coated barbarian had settled down and con-templated her options, I had fewer tasks to tend to. And that's when I finally opened my ears.

The captain was decidedly louder and angrier now than when he'd spoken earlier in the journey. The first thing I heard him say was "We're out of water."

The second was "Someone has stolen a piece of salted cod."

These two things left the other sailors silent with grave faces that slowly turned angry, as if an invisible hand were moving their skin and wrinkles around. Then began the fight that would leave our boat in more danger than we'd been in before.

Lucía, dropping all signs of compassion from the other night, rose up first in glorious fury and pointed at Heyu. "Haven't you been watching the food stores?"

"Yeah!" said Tembe accusingly, suddenly looking like he was sorry he'd helped the boy. I noticed for the first time that Tembe's shirt was in shreds, front and back, as if a giant Special Lady had raked her claws around him. But peeking between the rips in fabric were festering striped wounds that no cat could have caused. "He's our thief."

"I am not!" cried Heyu, his voice muffled. He took the poultice out of his mouth and struggled to sit up. "I can't even chew anything."

"Quiet!" roared the captain. He stood up in the boat. Sweat dripped from his forehead, and his once-tanned face was a deep crimson, redder than I'd ever seen it. His nose had a line of scabs running down it where the skin had blistered, and his lips were burned blue-black. The tops of his feet, once shockingly white, were bright red and peeling. "Whoever stole the food, confess now and take your punishment. Or I'll throw you all to the sharks one by one at my whim."

There was a moment of shocked silence, but the captain looked dead serious. And then more accusations started. Everyone began to argue. Some pleaded with the thief to speak up to save the innocent ones. Others pointed fingers and accused with ridiculous claims. "He's been sitting closest to that crate!" "She was sneaking toward the bow in the night!"

My eyes widened and my body froze. Someone innocent was going to take the blame for me stealing the salted cod. Just then the cat cast her tail into my sight line and reeled it back in. I crept forward and looked at her.

She was grinning, if you could call it that. Cheering on the chaos. And she was looking right at me. When the fight turned frenzied, the captain barked an order.

A moment later, two sailors hoisted Heyu up and sent

him overboard with a yelp. The splash reached us, and Special Lady retreated as far into the bow as she could fit, in case there was more coming.

Had they really thrown the boy out to drown? A lump throttled my throat. I despised Heyu for his noise, but I didn't feel right about him paying with his life for the fish I'd stolen. And I didn't want his half sister to lose him forever. Would I be responsible for murder? If so, my life's path had taken a sharp turn for the worse. It was an overwhelming feeling that made me want to confess.

Obviously they wouldn't understand my admission. They wouldn't believe it, either—no respectable mouse I knew would be caught dead with any part of a dried, salted fish in their mouth, unless they were starving. Moving those pieces to my stash had given me the horrors.

But . . . maybe the sailors would think to blame the cat, which didn't concern me in the slightest.

I strained to see. "I'm sorry, Heyu," I whispered as the splashing lessened from the boy and the outrage grew from within the boat. The sailors turned, protesting to the captain now, and the volume increased to a frenzy. It wasn't fair! It was murder! Where was the trial?

Finally Lucía threw one end of a rope overboard. She reeled in Heyu, who was choking and coughing. Tembe helped her drag him back into the launch. The boy collapsed at the bottom and lay with one ear in the dank sludge. He gasped for breath. I watched, fascinated and horrified, trying to comprehend this kind of cruelty. Had the last-minute rescue been planned all along? I didn't understand humans—the way they hurt one another to teach lessons. So many discussions led to shoving and yelling. Mice didn't behave that way. When your species is the kind that must fight to survive predators every moment of every day, you save your energy for that.

As Lucía and another sailor attended to Heyu, the rest continued sparring with the captain, which he didn't seem to appreciate. Some were still blaming him for being cruel, and others were coming to his defense, and just like that, it seemed like another mutiny was brewing. While they were all distracted, I crept through my crate to the slats to get a better view. A moment later, a shiver rippled down my spine as a whisker brushed my fur. I jumped, then slowly turned my head toward the cat, who perched on the triangular bow seat above me, within striking range.

She stretched her neck down toward me, and I froze. "Now," purred the monstrous Lady near my ear, "might be a good time to go after some more fish."

Not Long Now

"THAT'S NOT A terrible idea," I said cautiously, once I could breathe again after the shock of Special Lady speaking to me. But I was on high alert as I took the opportunity to steal more salted cod during the chaos. My fear was palpable as I crossed the open space between fish and safety, but Special Lady didn't come at me. It was my first victory against the world since the mutiny.

Unfortunately the salt startled my thirst and made it rage. Victories were fleeting when we didn't have fresh water.

"You're the only mouse here," Special Lady remarked when I finished the task.

It seemed sinister. "You're the only cat," I said. I felt like every word was a challenge.

"Your brother got away," she said. Her back leg shot out in front of her, startling me to retreat, but she merely began to lick her muddy fur and bite at her toe pads.

My brother. "What . . . happened?"

"An officer nabbed me before I could reach him. Threw me overboard like that sack of flour."

I gulped, halfway between fascinated and horrified, but also desperate to sound like I wasn't scared to death of her. I had to prove that I was the alpha mouse I'd portrayed myself to be. "Landed on your feet, I suppose," I said, slinking backward ever so slowly.

La Dame Spéciale gnawed and ripped some matted fur from between her toes. "Naturally," she growled.

THINGS SETTLED DOWN and another day passed without a cloud in the sky, and without a drop of water to drink. The sailors were slowly burning to a crisp under the fierce sun. Tembe crouched down with his shirt lifted over his head, trying to protect his burning skin. Lucía ripped open an empty sack and placed it over Heyu's head and shoulders to shield it. Only the captain seemed oblivious to the worsening burns and weeping sores on his body.

Special Lady came and went, never pouncing at me but also being just as creepy and untrustworthy as cats always are. With the afternoon sun striking my crate and heating it up, I panted, parched. Special Lady's tail hung from above, where she lounged on top of my crate, under the shade of the triangle seat. After a while, she got up and crept around the edges of the boat to the stern.

This time I watched carefully to see where her hiding place was. Mysteriously, perhaps magically, she went up on her hind legs and disappeared into a space under the transom that I couldn't see. No one paid any attention to her—clearly a benefit of being a cat. Imagine the ruckus if I'd done the same. When she came out a few moments later, her whiskers and nose were wet. I could see the sun reflecting off the drops. My tongue thickened just look-ing at them. She moved with care and stealth back to my crate. As I instinctively shrank into my knothole, she put her putrid fishy face against the slats, careful not to touch her whiskers to the wood. "Hurry up," she growled be-tween gritted teeth.

It startled me. At first I didn't understand what she wanted. But then I realized what she'd done. She'd brought me water. Just a few tiny drops on her whiskers.

"I . . . ," I said, overwhelmed. But . . . did she really expect me to get that close to her teeth? And was it fresh water? I took a few hesitant steps. I wanted to play this like I'd played her before, telling her who was boss. Telling her how tough I was, even though I'd been faking it.

But something had changed in our contentious relationship when the sailors had refused to offer her a ration of food. Something had shifted when the sailors had accused Heyu of stealing the salted cod. When they'd grown loud and out of control and reckless with their movements. And that thing had strengthened when the captain had ordered the cold act of throwing the galley boy to the sharks.

Special Lady was wise to it. Charles Sebastian, if he'd been here, would have seen it. But I was just figuring it out. The cat was no longer the captain's pet. She hadn't been, not since the mutiny. Not since the announcement of tight rations that didn't include her. She was a living creature requiring water and food, and had therefore become the captain's rival, just as each sailor was now a rival to the others.

The hard truth: No one wanted to feed the cat because it meant less for the humans. Special Lady was an animal, so her needs were less important to them than their own. Her complaints were less loud, her starvation less notable, less shocking than that of a sailor's.

She'd been forced to join my side.

With such limited food, no water, and no land in sight, it wouldn't be long before things grew dire. And Special

Lady needed an ally who would watch out for her. An invisible ally. Without water, this boundless journey might end sooner than anyone wanted.

Still, I was a helpless mouse and she was a sneaky cat, and I plainly didn't trust her and never would. There was no declaration of loyalty here. Try as I might, I couldn't muster up the bravado or arrogance I'd had the other day. I wanted those drops of water on my tongue badly, but my legs were shaking. "I'm afraid," I whispered. Putting it all out there. Ruining my alpha status. But it was all I had.

Special Lady closed her thin lips so her teeth weren't visible. Her tail curled around her bottom and remained there, not switching suspiciously. Her ears were up and forward, which I took as a sign of earnestness, and her eyes were half-closed. Accepting. She leaned closer.

I took the gift. The drops melted and spread across my tongue.

Afterward, when I'd retreated to safety, she told me the drops were from rainwater that had been trapped in a space inside the transom. Rain had seeped in through a crack and pooled there at the low end of the boat. Throughout the day she made three more trips, delivering fragments of rain to me until I was satisfied.

"Thank you," I said.

Special Lady narrowed her eyes as if she wasn't quite pleased with herself for what she was doing.

THAT NIGHT, WHEN all was calm except for the waves lapping against the hull and the two sailors on watch talking quietly at the sail, I ventured out to look at the blur of constellations. Somewhere out there, floating on the *Carlotta* under this same canopy, was Charles Sebastian. If he happened to be outside at this moment, was it possible that he and I could gaze upon the same stars? It made my brother seem closer to me. Connected. There was only the sky between us.

I missed my brother achingly. It was a slight comfort not to be totally alone against the world here in this crowded boat, though. To have a sort of ally. I didn't forget that this same cat had eaten Olivia and gone after Charles Sebastian, but I wasn't about to bring that up.

I wondered whether my brother was alone, or whether he'd found an ally, too.

A Flagrant Attack

CHARLES SEBASTIAN STUFFED what was left of the prize in today's successful biscuit-snatching into a space between deck boards at the back of the human's cage. He would return later to finish it. But now he needed water. He was feeling a bit of confidence, either from the act of poaching the ultimate enemy's food in broad daylight or from the swallows of grog. But the invisible belt that had cinched around his chest had broken loose, and he could breathe again. He looked at the prisoner and saw she was watching him. He lifted his nose. There was something thrilling about being so near a human who couldn't reach him.

"When the mice grow bold, a prisoner's fate's foretold," the girl muttered. Then she sighed. "I miss school. And my parents. I wish I'd never come." After a time she turned and eyed Charles Sebastian. "Is there a whole family of

you or are you one and the same? You look . . ." She wrinkled her nose. "Smaller."

Charles Sebastian didn't know what she meant. Perhaps
she'd seen Clarice or his mother or another mouse at some
point. "Smaller than what?" he piped, feeling especially
brave. The girl turned away, muttering her poetic couplet
again and moving her forefinger over the deck as if writing
out the lines.

The mouse eyed the path he'd taken before—the one
that led out of the pen and around the solid wall to the
other side, where the chicken coop was. Might he find
some water sitting out for them? If he could stay hidden,
he'd be able to have a look. He could always climb the wall
if Marigold or the chickens came at him. He spied a few
sailors near the railing, piling up coils of rope, but they
hadn't noticed him.

Before Charles Sebastian could take a step, a huge
shadow rolled over him. He flattened in fear.

"Albatross," one of the sailors mused, squinting up at
the top of the mizzenmast where the bird landed. "That
means good luck."

Charles Sebastian didn't know whether the albatross
was a predator or not, but it didn't seem to care about him.
So that definitely felt like good luck. Keeping an eye on it

overhead, Charles Sebastian bolted out of the human's cage and headed for the chicken coop, then stopped abruptly just outside the corner, feeling like everything around him was too big. As he did so, an officer approached the ones at the railing. The group pointed out the bird to one another as if it were something notable.

"What do you reckon, Mr. Thomas?" said one sailor. "Albatross." Mr. Thomas was the head mutineer who'd ordered the captain into the boat.

"Hey," shouted Benjelloun at the new acting captain. "Let me out of here! I didn't do anything wrong!"

"Quiet, you insubordinate sneak," said Mr. Thomas haughtily. "Never speak to me."

"But you've got me out here exposed to the weather. That's not safe."

"Safe!" The man laughed. "What makes you think I want to keep you safe after what you did?"

Benjelloun glared. The other sailors glanced uneasily at one another.

"Besides," Mr. Thomas went on, "you have shade from the sun and a starry night view, princess. Fresh air, too—much better than being stuck in the brig with the unsavory characters down there." He paused, glancing up at the albatross. "Maybe this experience will teach you to keep your nose out of the first officer's business."

"You're making a big mistake, punishing me extra hard because you think I heard what you said," Benjelloun warned. "Maybe I did. Maybe you'll hang because of me."

Mr. Thomas flinched. "You might want to think twice about who you're threatening, sailor." He turned sharply and started away from the cage, his face flooding with anger. He looked over his shoulder at the others. "Don't kill the albatross, that's what I reckon," the man said through gritted teeth, as if trying to recover from his fit of anger at a twelve-year-old. "Or we might lose our good fortune."

"Hey!" cried Benjelloun again. "Let me off the ship with the rest of them, and I won't say a word." But Mr. Thomas strode away.

Charles Sebastian used that distraction to dart around to the other side of the wall, going so fast he bumped into a wooden bowl of water, making some of it splash out. After stopping for a long drink, he continued around to the front of the coop, remembering the straw he'd failed to collect last time. He hesitated at the ramp and peered in. He didn't see any of the feathery heads or pointy beaks. He skittered up and went inside, finding the coop empty. The chickens were out roaming. Or terrorizing was more like it. There were three perfect brown eggs in the straw near one corner.

Charles Sebastian heard a ruckus outside and peeked

around, terrified. Were the chickens returning? But no, it was the group of sailors moving a little too close for comfort, working the ropes that controlled the sails right outside the coop. Slowly, Charles Sebastian backed into a corner and made himself small, stuck there until the sailors left. Perhaps the chickens wouldn't return with all this racket going on. After a moment, the little mouse poked his nose beneath the straw and moved it around to form a softer bed. After so many days in damp, uncomfortable places, the straw made him feel cozy. While he waited, he fell into the deepest sleep he'd had in a long while.

When he awoke to his fur standing up, the noise of the sailors had gone. But a crazy-eyed chicken was staring down at him, her beak mere inches from Charles Sebastian's vulnerable eyes. She struck out and pecked his head, then grabbed his ear and lifted him up by it. Pain tore through Charles Sebastian's head, and he squealed in agony. The chicken's sharp beak ripped through the ear. She dropped him, and he tried to run. But the bird struck again, snapping her jaws around the mouse's middle and lifting him up. He could see her wattle flapping.

Charles Sebastian's ear throbbed. Blood burned and ran down into his eye. He squealed and squirmed, swiping his claws at the chicken's face. Then he wriggled loose from her grip and fell with a thud onto the coop's floor. He scrambled, unable to gain traction on the loose straw, then darted forward and reached the ramp, falling and rolling down it.

When he found his feet, he bolted back to safety around the wall and squeezed flat in the corner of the human's cage. His chest pounded, and his breath snarled around his bruised sides. Blood blinded him. He shivered in place for a long time, wishing for his sister, his big bean, to cuddle him and remind him that everything was going to be okay.

The words of the two whispering sailors from days ago returned to him. They were going to look for the others on the captain's launch boat. He would have a chance to find his sister.

Then he thought of Clarice's promise and her belief in him. Perhaps she'd seen in him what he'd only just begun noticing about himself. Slowly, with trembling paws, Charles Sebastian started to clean his wounded ear and prepare for whatever trial came next.

A Sign

THE INCIDENT WITH Heyu and the missing food was the prelude to something dreadful.

With no water, life quickly became unbearable. By the end of the first waterless day, things were testy. After the second, the sailors went silent, perhaps preserving whatever moisture they could on their tongues. They positioned themselves to shield one another from the afternoon sun, but its rays were relentless. The sailors scanned the skies, and their furrowed brows prayed for rain.

Heyu became very ill. His face was distorted beyond recognition, infected, bloated with pus. The near-drowning had worsened his condition, and he lay unmoving at the bottom of the boat. His odor changed. I feared he wasn't long for this world.

"You nearly killed him," Lucía whispered to the captain. She'd been furious with the man for ordering Heyu to be thrown overboard. "That was cruel. Unnecessary. Do you question why there was a mutiny?"

"Are you accusing me of attempted murder?" asked the captain, incredulous and arrogant even as he faced thirsting to death.

"*I* am," Tembe declared, backing up Lucía.

"Stand down," one of the captain's supporters said to the two.

"I will speak up against injustice," Lucía said evenly, eyeing the supporter.

The man's eyes flared, but he had no answer. "Stop wasting my time," he muttered, and turned his back on her.

The captain remained silent, but his face exploded in anger. Tembe and Lucía stopped responding to the captain, as if daring him to do something about them, and the rest of the crew was caught in the middle. Uneasy. Shifty-eyed. Things were bad. But the imminent tragic ending of life gave some of them new boldness. They had little to lose.

I glanced at Special Lady. Her eyes were like slits, watching the affair. Whose side did she take? I wasn't sure whether she still felt loyalty to the captain or if she now despised him as much as I did. Heyu had often fed her in the past, so she might be partial to him. But he'd stopped, so perhaps she had no sympathy for his situation. I was more than curious but afraid to start a conversation with the cat. I hadn't forgotten that she could end my life in a single turn.

Our wariness of each other was verging on the cold side of respect. I fed her, she watered me. But our water supply was drying up quickly. We all needed a good drenching if we were to survive. Unfortunately, the sky was clear and the sun continued brutally roasting the sailors. Despite their efforts, they were covered in burns and blisters and sores from overexposure. The stench grew.

We would not last much longer before our boat became a morgue.

If they all died, how long could a mouse and cat live together on a boat that was aimlessly floating wherever the sail decided to turn? With no one to bail out the seawater?

"What do you expect will happen?" I ventured when the cat remained quiet.

"They'll toss them overboard once they're dead," Special Lady guessed. "That'll lighten the load and keep the sea from breaching."

"And when they are too weak to lift the dead?"

"Only the last few will remain." Her whiskers twitched.

And then what?

It seemed morbid to talk like that, yet here we were,

on the brink of expiration. Both of us were familiar with death. One false move. One bad storm. One human snatching you up and changing the course of your life in an instant. One more day without water, and things would spiral rapidly to a painful, purposeless end.

One more day and it would be the beginning of the end for them. And then for us.

Unless it rained.

WE DOZED ON and off. It was a relief to have everyone keeping quiet. Sometime in the middle of the night, we were jolted awake. The sailor who'd stood up against Lucía and Tembe was stumbling over the bodies, moving away from us. He tripped and fell, and when he turned his face to the moonlight, his expression was one I'd never seen before—eyes bulging, mouth frothing. His breath was ragged as if he'd been running. "Give me water," he whispered, his words catching and unraveling in his throat. He lunged at the sleeping captain, who woke in an instant and shoved the sailor away.

"You've gone mad!" the captain said. Others stirred and sat up, bewildered.

"He's mad," Tembe repeated to the ones just waking up. "Everyone on your guard." The sailor came at the captain again, and the captain punched him in the jaw, sending the madman reeling and tripping backward over Lucía. He hit his lower back on the gunwale and nearly flipped into the sea, but Lucía lunged for his leg and held him in. He kicked and struggled, kneeing her in the nose and back-handing another sailor in the chin. That sailor reared up, closed-fisted and ready to fight.

I shrank back into the point of the bow, and Special Lady slinked down and slid back, too. Heyu, unconscious, got trampled, and the brawl grew. Two others went flipping over the gunwales into the water. They struggled to get back into the boat, screaming that they couldn't swim.

"They can't swim?" I marveled. "What madness to become sailors without that knowledge!"

"They'll learn any moment," Special Lady said sarcastically.

Soon everyone was yelling and brawling. The captain, Lucía, and Tembe tried to get control, but it took a long time. Everyone was thirsty and exhausted. The sailor who'd started this mess ended up drinking handful after handful of seawater. He wouldn't stop. He couldn't.

"That will make him more mad," Special Lady informed me, as if she'd witnessed this before. "He's not long for this world now. It won't be pretty."

"How do you know?" I ventured.

"I saw it a few years ago. My sister and I—" She stopped abruptly and frowned.

I didn't dare inquire further. Instead I watched, fear knotted in my gut, as the crew tried to pull themselves together and treat the one who'd gone mad from thirst. But he was far gone. "There's land," he kept croaking, though it was dark and impossible to see. His speech was thick and hard to understand. He kept trying to get out of the launch, causing more water to spill in and requiring more people to bail the water out when their muscles couldn't function properly. Some of them cried out in agony. It was a scene I never wish to relive.

By morning they'd successfully tied the man down. I couldn't erase the look or sound of him: eyes sunk into his skull, breath labored. And he gurgled—a strange, unsettling noise I'd never heard before and never wanted to hear again. It was just a matter of time.

Then, when things finally went quiet, we heard another throat rattling. This time it was Heyu. Lucía roused and checked him over, held his wrist, touched his neck. After a long while she looked up, hard, at the captain. Then she said with contempt, "He's dead."

A pang of sorrow seared through me—not for myself,

but for Benjelloun, who might never know what happened to him. Would my experience with my brother mirror hers? I glanced at the cat, who got up and tentatively made the rounds, sniffing at everything that was . . . different.

Not a moment later, while Lucía and the captain were still glaring at each other, radiating tension from every inch of their blistered, mottled skin, we heard the call of a seagull.

At once, all the sailors turned toward it. As the sun scraped the sky's edge, we saw a rocky island rising up in the distance. "Land!"

Worse Than Before

I SNUCK OUT to watch as they buried the two dead sailors at sea, sending them underwater off the coast of Kingsland . . . or what the humans assumed was Kingsland. It was disconcerting to see Heyu and the other man slip away under the liquid that reflected the blue sky, like they were passing through colored glass. The waves didn't splash in as much after that, and I went back to my hiding place, feeling a bit wrecked over it all. The captain bent over his journal, sighed, and wrote something down.

With a surge of energy, sailors began to paddle with the oar and their arms toward the rocky shore, impatient to find fresh water and step onto solid ground. I'd never seen land before—I'd only heard my mother's stories. I had no idea land would be so vast and overwhelming. Not at all flat like a deck. It was infinitely larger than the ship, and very intimidating. Was that why my mother had preferred the sea?

We dropped anchor in a shallow lagoon not far from the rocky shore. The captain studied the landscape with a consternated look on his face.

"There's no one here," Lucía said uneasily. "No structures. No sign of habitation. Are you sure this is Kingsland?"

"No," said the captain. "This is nothing like what I remember. Perhaps we're on a different side of it." He was silent for a long moment as the other sailors muttered under their breath.

"We should go ashore," said one.

"At least look for water," begged another.

"Quiet," said the captain. "I can't think straight."

Under the broiling sun, the sailors' impatience and thirst melted together to form a sort of heavy desperation. Finally, the captain gave in. "I don't want to bring the launch any closer. Let's disembark here and search for fresh water. Leave the barrel behind until we know where to find it—there's no sense wasting our energy dragging that around."

"You heard the captain." Lucía stood up, her eyes roaming the hull and coming to a stop on my old crate. "Someone grab the coffee beans and flour," she ordered, "in case anyone is there to trade with. All right, sir?"

"Yes," said the captain. "Of course." I was glad they

were talking to each other again. I retreated when someone grabbed the sacks of flour and coffee, then came back out to watch them disembark.

A man called Silveridge grunted and eased into the water, waist-deep. Lucía handed him the sacks, and he carried them carefully balanced, one on each shoulder. Special Lady and I crouched in the bow and waited. A woman had been ordered to stay behind with the launch, and she sat near the stern.

Special Lady could see the captain, Lucía, and the rest of them approach the shore, and in her quiet, chittering way, she told me what was happening. "They're onshore now," she said. "Heading to the trees."

"All together?" I asked.

"Yes. Staying in a group."

"That seems wise."

"Now they're gone from sight," said the cat. "I can still see the leaves moving." She shifted her hind legs, then got up and jumped down to strut along the gunwales— something she hadn't felt free to do with so many sailors around to knock her into the water.

The sailor in the boat strained to see any sort of action onshore, and with her preoccupation, I took the opportunity to sneak more salted cod into my stash. I pulled out another fragment of a biscuit as well.

The sky overhead was clear and blue. No sign of rain. Special Lady returned, arched her back, then settled down again to watch. I dozed.

My nap was interrupted by shouts, followed by an ear-rattling *bang* that split the air. Special Lady and I both jumped, and the sailor with us gasped and sat up, on high alert.

"What's going on?" I whispered.

"I don't see anything," Special Lady said. We heard more shouting but couldn't make out the words.

"Dear God," said the sailor, jumping to her feet. She went to the anchor rope and peered out to see if anyone was coming.

"The tree leaves are moving," Special Lady reported. Then, "The captain just burst out from the foliage. And the others! They're running toward us."

"Do they have water?"

"They're not carrying anything," said Special Lady.

"Not the coffee beans and flour?"

"Not so far." She frowned.

"What is it?" I asked.

"Someone's missing."

"What's happening?" cried the sailor in the boat.

Special Lady hopped off the triangle bench and

slithered back into the corner underneath it, her eyes wide and ears flat.

"What's happening?" I asked, echoing the sailor. I could hear thunderous splashing.

Then the captain shouted, "Pull the anchor!" Seconds later, the boat tipped wildly as sailors clambered in. I was launched from my spot.

"Go! Go! Go!" shouted Lucía from the water. "Hurry!" She waited until everyone was in, then shoved the boat, swimming with it, trying to give it a start, but it didn't help much. Then she climbed in, too. Others began paddling with the oar and their arms while someone worked the sail.

"What about Silveridge?" Tembe asked the captain, sounding furious. "We're just going to leave him?"

"He's dead," growled the captain. "Shove on."

The sailors rowed with all the strength they had, passing the oar when their muscles gave out, until we were far from the island and the winds grabbed the sail.

"Someone please tell me what happened," demanded the sailor who'd stayed in the launch.

No one spoke at first. Finally the captain lifted his head. "That wasn't Kingsland."

"The inhabitants were not pleased to see us," said Lucía.

"I think we surprised them. They had weapons . . . and took our supplies. Tembe nearly got struck."

Tembe nodded grimly. "Silveridge went down. He was next to me."

"He's dead," the captain said again, as if trying to convince himself. Uncertainty hung in the air, moving between parties like a swarm of gnats. But no one challenged the statement, at least not at first.

Tembe narrowed his eyes and stared at the bottom of the boat. "It was his shoulder bleeding."

"His chest," said the captain. "Certain death."

Tembe moved away abruptly to where Lucía sat, near us. "He was alive," he whispered.

"I know."

Special Lady heard them, too. We exchanged a glance. The captain pulled out his journal, and as he wrote, he muttered the date, then: "Attempted approach on apparently deserted rocky island." He used one of his tools to determine the coordinates of their location, then wrote that down, too. After a moment's pause, he continued, with everyone looking on: "Mr. Silveridge succumbed to injuries inflicted by the island's people. The rest of us fled for our lives to the launch." He closed the journal.

Tembe turned away in disgust and exhaustion. Lucía stared hard at the captain. Nobody said a word.

The captain had lied. And they'd left one of their sailors behind to fend for himself.

I shivered at the callousness.

"If we can just make it to Kingsland," the captain said after a while, "we'll get healthy. Then we'll secure a ride back home on a proper ship so we can report the mutineers."

"We can't be far off now," muttered Tembe. His voice was pleading, and it broke as he said it. He put his face in his hands.

"A few days," barked the captain.

Lucía rested a hand on Tembe's shoulder to comfort him, but she continued to glare at the captain. "Some of us haven't got a few days left."

From Afar

CHARLES SEBASTIAN'S EAR had been ripped in two.

It stopped bleeding eventually, but it throbbed and ached for days. He could tell that it wasn't growing back together, and the separation unsettled him. That chicken had taken a chunk right out of it. But it made him feel— what was the word he wanted—*seasoned. Battle-scarred.* Even . . . *accomplished.* "You were right about the chickens, Mother," Charles Sebastian confirmed to the air. He was glad to still have his eyes.

The prisoner noticed his injury when he came looking for crumbs. "Did you have a run-in with Marigold?" she asked.

"It was Mabel," he said, correcting her even though she wouldn't understand him. "The chicken."

She narrowed her eyes and peered closer, grudgingly impressed. "You survived, though. Not bad." She shook her head slightly, sizing him up. "When the mice grow bold . . ." She held out her empty hands to him. The ropes had turned her wrists raw. "Come closer. Come on, mousie. I'm bored."

Charles Sebastian stayed in the corner. "Humans are bad news," he told her. "They are the worst enemy." Still, he held his head higher—the girl's words of praise buoyed him. He'd survived a chicken attack. He still didn't trust anyone or anything, but there was a feeling of safety in this cage. The chickens were too skittish to come between the bars. The cats weren't, but they mostly slithered and crept about belowdecks—Charles Sebastian hadn't seen Special Lady since the night of the mutiny, and he didn't miss her.

The sailors didn't come inside the human's cage, either. There was only the prisoner in chains to worry about, and she couldn't go far. "At least I can tell you apart from the rest of the scavengers now, with that ear," the girl muttered. She sat back with a soft *hff* and began to work on more poetry, which she made up to pass the time. "Albatross. Cross. Doss. Across. Moss. Toss."

Charles Sebastian knew this kind of human vocalizing was unimportant. As he nibbled at the biscuit he'd stored between the deck boards, he let his mind wander to the important kind of words—the kind to which his ears would immediately attune. Whispered or shouted words, like *mutiny. Fire. Hurricane. Cat.* And *chicken.* Chickens were strutting about the area now, making Charles Sebastian very uneasy.

He finished his biscuit and tried to swallow the last bits that glopped onto the back of his tongue. He was going to have to find water elsewhere. Or learn to like the grog.

When the girl dozed off, her finger still pointed like a pencil to write invisible words on wood, Charles Sebastian tipped her cup over and got a few sips in as she woke with a start. "You're going to need to stop doing that," she said, annoyed. He retreated. She glared at him in his corner for a long moment, then softened slightly. "I imagine you're just thirsty." But she drained the few drops left in her cup. "You've got the run of the ship. Can't you find your own grog?"

"It's not that easy," Charles Sebastian muttered. Humans never understood anything. But he began to measure distances with his eyes. Maybe he'd have to step outside his comfort zone and go back to the coop. If only the chickens would go away.

When a sailor came to collect the girl's plate and cup, she stopped him. "Where are we?" she whispered.

He looked over his shoulder, then whispered back, "Heading for the atolls. Should be there tomorrow. We'll drop off the lot of loyalists and stay a few nights so we don't look suspicious. Stock up on a few things, like water and produce. Then we'll be on our way to find—" He stopped short. "Never mind."

"To find the other secret mutineers in the launch," Benjelloun said, rolling her eyes. "I know. Why do you think I'm stuck in prison?" She huffed, then sat back. "Is there any chance at all that Mr. Thomas will let me go ashore?"

"Come on, Benjelloun," the man scoffed. "You're dangerous to him."

"I only want to find Theo."

"Who?"

"The kitchen boy," the girl said impatiently. "I'm sure he has no idea about your plans."

"Oh, him. No one knew his name."

Benjelloun wrinkled her forehead and sat back. "That's very rude."

Charles Sebastian and the rest of his family had thought his name was Heyu. But now the mouse was struck with the realization that it was only the cook shouting "Hey, you!"

The sailor stared quizzically at the girl. "He's your brother? That's rotten luck. To be separated, I mean," he added hastily.

"*Half* brother. Can you convince Mr. Thomas? Or let me speak to him again? I'll be respectful this time. I'll tell him I've learned my lesson."

"Obviously there's no chance Thomas will let you off the ship. He can't risk having you tell anybody where we're headed. I'm afraid you're stuck in prison until we get there."

Benjelloun gripped her hair in frustration. "I give you my word! I promise not to tell. I—I didn't even hear it."

"You just confessed otherwise." The sailor shook his head in disbelief. He looked over his shoulder again, then leaned in. "They'll torture it out of you on the mainland if the captain finds you, and you'll be forced to testify against Mr. Thomas. You shouldn't have joked about that—he's not going to forget it."

"I wasn't joking," Benjelloun muttered.

"Well, you're going to the . . . the *place* . . . with us. And you'll be staying there. So you might want to work on getting along with Mr. Thomas instead of fighting him."

The girl closed her eyes in defeat, and the sailor looked on with a note of sympathy. "Have you got other family or something?" he asked gruffly. "Besides . . . the kitchen boy?"

Benjelloun hung her head. "Yes. My mother and father. They'll die of sadness if they never see me again. Unless . . ."

"What?"

"Mother's been lost at sea, so we don't know when . . . or if . . . she'll return. Father's ship was delayed coming in, and there's no guarantee he has returned home, either. Now Theo and I are separated." She shook her head miserably. "All four of us in different places. I don't think we'll ever . . ." She stifled a sob with a snort, as if angry it escaped.

"I'm . . . sorry."

"Sure. No one here gives a rat's tail about me."

Charles Sebastian's eyes widened at the image.

The man turned to go. As he locked the cage door, the girl looked up. "Could you at least bring me a cup of water with my meal?"

"Instead of the grog?"

"In addition to it," she said.

"You aren't allowed both."

Benjelloun swore. "Look. You've got me sweltering in the weather all day. You'll stock up on plenty of fresh water when we stop at the atolls."

"Most of that will be for the saplings." He rolled his eyes. "Precious cargo."

"It's the least you can do. You know I've done nothing except be in the wrong place at the wrong time. I barely overheard anything Thomas was saying."

"You heard enough to cause serious trouble for all of us." He rattled the door to make sure it was secure. As he walked away, he looked over his shoulder. "I'll see what I can do."

THE NEXT DAY, the man brought a cup of water with him in addition to the rest. When Benjelloun finished her meal, she frowned and glanced at the corner where Charles Sebastian usually stayed. She poured a little of the water onto her plate and pushed it as far as her tethered hands could manage, toward that corner. Then she slid over the other way as much as the ankle chains would allow. Taking her watered-down grog in both hands to sip, she waited. Not looking at the mouse.

Charles Sebastian was smart enough to know that the man would soon return to pick up the plate. The torn pieces of his ear tremored a warning like a divining rod, but he'd seen how Benjelloun was. He could sense her ways. Humans were the worst enemies, but this girl was different. She was gruff but gentle, and it didn't seem like she would hurt him.

He crept forward, keeping an eye on her, and drank gratefully from the plate.

THE NEXT DAY, the ship stopped pressing onward and rocked side to side instead. Different sounds were all around. Birds and voices—cheerful voices, not like the angry sailors'. Charles Sebastian climbed the mizzenmast to see what was happening. With wonder, he could make out the hustle and bustle of a busy seaport—something he'd never seen before. He observed as some of the sailors brought out small trees in large pots from a part of the ship he hadn't been to. They'd be trading them for water and goods.

He watched the activity for a while, then got down and roamed the ship, staying out of the way of the remaining sailors, cats, and chickens, and listened from between spokes in the railing as Thomas and the others bartered for the goods and supplies they wanted.

Right before they set sail again, the mutineers let off the ones who'd been loyal to the captain but couldn't fit in the launch. They would stay here, in the atolls, until the next friendly ship made a stop and offered to take them back to the mainland.

When the ship grew quiet, Benjelloun wept.

Then she gave the mouse her water again.

The Worst of Times

THE MORALE IN the launch was the lowest it had ever been. Everyone's eyes were sunken, their bones sticking out. There was a bit of beef left in the barrel, but the brine was so salty it only made the sailors thirstier. The crumbs of hard tack were like paste in their throats, choking them with nothing to wash it down. They lost their appetites. Another sailor went mad, and by the end of that day, the body went over the side, released by sailors whose breath was labored. They were barely able to lift it.

"The water is gone," Special Lady reported. "Dried up in the heat."

"Do you sense rain?"

"No. Do you?"

I wanted to. "Maybe," I said to keep hope alive. I breathed in, feeling the dry air irritating my nostrils. We stayed in our places, unmoving, not speaking, to preserve our inner moisture. It's an instinct with animals. Somehow we know how to survive the harshest elements. We knew we'd be the last ones alive on this launch. But then what? I eyed Special Lady. If it were a contest, she'd win.

Another day, and everyone hovered just above death. Even the captain had gone silent. Lucía and the woman who'd stayed with the launch at the island were the most lucid and did what they could for the others to make them comfortable. There wasn't much.

They were hours away from their bodies shutting down for good when the air changed. The sea turned choppy. The sky streaked with lightning—enough to see a sky full of dark clouds. Lucía, her lips cracked and bleeding, her face gaunt, sat up and looked out. Special Lady crept out from under our cover to look, too. I sniffed. The air was moist.

"There's rain," Lucía rasped, her voice like burning coals being raked in the stove. "Just there. I can see the line. Tembe, help me. Watson, look alive. Be ready to switch out."

Lucía and Tembe used the paddle together, moving in slow motion as their bodies allowed, trying to get to the rain. Soon the other woman eased over to the center to relieve Tembe. "Steady now," Lucía said between huffs. "Pull."

I heard the first drop hit. Then another, and then a pattering. The sailors stopped rowing and reached for the empty vessels they'd prepared for this purpose weeks ago.

Special Lady and I didn't waste a moment. She jumped to the spot above my head and began lapping up the drops. I stood under the lip of the seat and let the water drip down on my nose and mouth. It spread over my tongue and soothed my throat. I could feel it travel all the way to my stomach. It was glorious and fresh and perfect and everything we needed. I drank until I could have burst, and wished for a vessel of my own to fill.

Special Lady disappeared to her secret spot and returned after a while. "Our reservoir is filling back up," she reported. "The slant of the rain is right."

Our.

I was moved by her inclusion. "I'm grateful for that," I said when I found my voice. "And . . . for you." I felt suddenly shy but pushed forward before I regretted it. "If you hadn't shared your water, I'd be long dead."

"And I'd be starving," said Special Lady. "I'm grateful, too." She suddenly had an itch in between her paw pads and attacked it with fervor.

LATELY I'D BEEN thinking about what would happen to me if we made it to land. If food and water were plentiful once more, would the cat's natural drive for sport resurface? Neither of us ever raised the question of whether our little arrangement, born of necessity, was permanent or temporary. But I often wondered. Perhaps we'd go our separate ways immediately and I was worried for nothing. But even with a full, sloshing belly, I wasn't about to let my guard down. I slid a hunk of salted cod through the slats so it would be ready for her when she felt like having it. An offering to the cat, and a nod to the rain gods. Special Lady was the healthiest of all of us, and I hoped she wouldn't forget how that had come to be.

To the Brink

THE RAIN SAVED most of them. With water came energy, and with energy came hunger and renewed arguments over food rations. "We should be allowed to have a little more than before," Lucía argued with the captain. "We've fewer mouths to feed now. And we need to get our strength back."

"We don't know how long we'll be out here," the captain argued.

"But you keep saying we're just a few days from Kingsland," Tembe pointed out.

"Something's off," said the captain in a low voice. "By my calculations we've sailed over it multiple times by now."

"We should aim for somewhere else, then," stressed Lucía. "Why aren't we looking for another civilized island?"

"Are we just going around in circles?" asked Tembe, in- credulous.

It seemed obvious to me that they'd be able to tell just by looking at the position of the sun every morning. But then again, Tembe was often on night watch and slept in bits and pieces during the day, so maybe he hadn't no- ticed. Not to mention the lack of water had seemed to cause a lot of confusion for everyone this week.

"Of course not," said the captain. "How dare you ques- tion my methods!"

"I dare because my life depends on finding land," Tembe retorted.

Lucía let a fist fly at Tembe's face and caught him in the jaw. "You won't speak to the captain like that."

Tembe reared back in surprise, then put a hand to his face. He didn't say anything else, though he looked angry. Those two were thick as thieves, and the action came as a surprise to me and Special Lady, too.

"Did she just do that?" I whispered.

"She did indeed," murmured the cat.

Lucía looked away.

The captain gave Tembe a disdainful glance. "I don't think you want to join the mutineers in the gallows, do you?"

Tembe looked shocked. Finally he found his tongue. "Of course not, Captain," he said. The words came out thick and oily.

Later, when Tembe was asleep, Lucía spoke quietly to the captain. "You have to tell me your plan here," she said, sounding angry with him. "How much longer are you going to comb this area before we start looking for someplace else?"

"Kingsland is our best option," the captain argued. "It's safe, the people there are fond of me, food and water are plentiful, and ships stop frequently. We'll be able to make safe passage home quickly to report the crime."

"If so many other ships can find it, why can't we?" Lucía said. "Are you remembering the coordinates wrong? If so, we'll never locate it. We'll die out here!"

The captain snarled. "I'll find it," he said.

"When?" demanded Lucía, loud enough to make a few others turn to look, fear in their eyes.

"I'll find it when I *want* to find it!"

What a ridiculous thing to say. The woman glared at him. There was no love lost between them, that much we already knew. And while Lucía, one of the ship's senior officers, had been loyal to the captain, she was clearly running out of patience. This maniacal situation that the stubborn captain was putting everyone in seemed like it could cause another split. Only this time, there would be only six sailors involved. And there wasn't an extra boat in which to set the captain adrift.

Meanwhile, my heart longed for my brother. And my mind spun with memories of that fateful night we were separated. How I wish I'd followed him. I'd hidden when I should have run. Would I ever get it right? Mother's words echoed in my ears. But my doubts were louder today.

I missed them so much—Mother and Olivia and Charles Sebastian. Feeling sad, I rested my chin on my paws and sighed.

"Everything all right?" Special Lady asked.

I glanced up, having forgotten she was there. "I miss my family."

"That's . . . too bad."

I frowned. It was an unusual thing to say, considering she'd eaten one of them. After a while, I began to wonder if there was anyone Special Lady was missing, too.

Mutual Disgust

THE *CARLOTTA* SAILED away from the grand port in the atolls, leaving the captain's supporters behind except for Benjelloun, who remained imprisoned for the act of being within hearing range when someone said something incriminating. Surely now that the loyalists were gone, Thomas would let Benjelloun out—there was no one left to tell of Thomas's secret plans but the people who were in on it. Yet, Mr. Thomas was quick to hold a grudge.

As much as Charles Sebastian despised humans, he was starting to think the young one had promise, and he felt like this was a travesty.

The cats, however, seemed thrilled by the shipboard changes. "The pantry door was left open this morning," Marigold told Robin as the two crossed paths on the upper deck, not far from where Charles Sebastian was hiding. "Did you notice?"

"Not enough sailors left to run the ship properly," Robin

said, sounding a bit haughty. He was black and white and appeared to be wearing a mask. Marigold was a yellower shade of orange than Special Lady. The two touched noses and went their separate ways. Benjelloun called to the cats, begging them to come to her so she could pet them, but they ignored her. The girl watched them go, crestfallen.

Charles Sebastian felt otherwise. "Where *is* Special Lady?" he wondered aloud as he nibbled on a sharp corner of wood to keep his teeth in top shape. He hadn't seen the cat since she'd chased him out of the crate.

An unexpected pang seared through him at the memory. If only he'd stayed in the crate instead of running. He'd caused this separation. But why hadn't Clarice run, too? The cat was *upon* them! It made no sense to him. It never had.

Around him, Mr. Thomas and the rest of the mutineers grew raucous and gleeful now that there were no more loyalists to contend with. But they also whispered and worried. *What if the captain survives and comes after us?* Charles Sebastian reasoned that if he did, it would only increase the odds of him finding Clarice, so he was all for it.

In contrast to the boisterous sailors, Benjelloun grew somber. Deflated. Perhaps she'd given up. Charles Sebastian watched her more closely. It had never occurred to him before to help a human—the thought was ludicrous. Enemy number one and all that. Not to mention, he'd sort of been used to others helping *him* all his life. Yet, Benjelloun had done so much for him. She'd allowed him to take food and had gotten him water so he could stay in the safety of the cage. Now that his battle scars were healing and he was feeling stronger in his own abilities, he wondered what, if anything, a tiny mouse could do for such a girl.

With fewer sailors around to do the daily tasks, the chickens were neglected. They clucked and squawked and fluttered all around, muttering like birdbrains about wanting the captain to return. Apparently the newly restocked pantry didn't translate to more chicken feed, and the mean birds grew more demanding. The attack chicken often wandered by the human's cage in search of food.

On this turn, she poked her head and neck between the bars. She squawked and clucked at Benjelloun as if expecting the young sailor to feed her. Soon the other chickens joined, and a couple of them pushed in. Charles Sebastian's pulse raced as visions of attacking chickens haunted him. He burrowed into the space between boards on the back wall and trembled. He stroked his ripped ear, trying to soothe his worries. The ear felt rough and itchy as it healed.

Benjelloun, who'd been lying on her side next to her

plate and mugs, wrapped her arms around her head. "Quiet," she muttered. "I don't have your food." She shooed them into the corner, but the squawking grew louder and more insistent. Benjelloun threw the inedible food scraps at the chickens to drive them away—a small hunk of cheese rind and the moldy peel of a rotting orange. Charles Sebastian closed his eyes in defeat. Tossing food only served to encourage the birds as they fought over the scraps that should have gone to him. The mouse's eardrums were growing numb from the noise. There was nothing he could do to help this situation.

Benjelloun poured a bit of water onto her plate as usual, then glanced to the empty spot in the wall where Charles Sebastian often rested. "Where are you, you little runt? Chickens have you worried?" She made a chirping noise—the same noise she'd used to try to coax the cats over.

Charles Sebastian's whiskers turned up. She was chirping for him. Perhaps it was the only animal call she knew. It felt good to be called, and it warmed him through. But even though he was thirsty, he couldn't venture out for a drink with the chickens so close.

When the sailor came to pick up the plate, Benjelloun refused to slide it through the space under the door. "I'm not finished," she said.

The sailor frowned. "It's empty. The food's gone. Cook needs the plate for sailors' grub."

"You've only got half the crew you used to," she argued. "Don't tell me this plate is so important. Besides, I'm still a sailor, whether you let me work or not. And I'm keeping it." Benjelloun averted her eyes and turned her sullen gaze to the deck while the never-ending scolding of the chickens grew louder. "Clear these stupid chickens out of here," she growled. "Feed them, for God's sake. They're driving me mad."

"That's not my job," said the sailor, annoyed.

"It's the job of the cook's apprentice, but he's serving his captain, like I should be." Spit flew from Benjelloun's lips. She wiped her mouth on her sleeve.

"Somebody else does that job now," the man said weakly.

"Not very well," said Benjelloun. "Let me out of here and I'll feed them."

Frustrated, the sailor kicked at the nearest hen, scaring the bunch out of the human's cage, and left without the plate. The chickens scattered, then roamed the deck. Benjelloun threw her arms over her ears again and curled up on her side.

Later, the sailor stumped up to the cage, arms laden with a burlap sack that smelled of chicken feed. He dropped it, then unlocked the door. "All right, sailor," he said, coming in with the key to the shackles. "I convinced Thomas we need more help. And I suggested it might be even more of a punishment to put you to work, so don't look like you're enjoying it. The rest of the time, you'll be back in here like usual. Thomas said he won't put up with you sneaking around listening to his conversations." He knelt to unlock the shackles and untie the rope around her wrists.

Benjelloun stared. Tears came to her eyes. "Thank you," she said.

"Now get to work," the sailor said, standing up and heading out. "You can start with the chickens."

BENJELLOUN RETURNED FROM her shift, limping and carrying a cup. Once she was shackled and tied and the sailor had gone, she poured water onto the plate she'd kept and lay on the deck, exhausted. "Tough day," she said in the direction of Charles Sebastian's hiding spot. "I'm happy I got out, but Thomas has it in for me. Hauled ropes and swabbed decks . . . My whole body hurts." She closed her eyes. "Thomas told me I'll never go home again."

Charles Sebastian's heart twisted. "That's a terrible thing to say, even if it's true," he squeaked. He sampled the air from his hiding place and reached out a paw to stretch. Then he crept stiffly onto the deck, looking carefully behind him for chickens. He inched toward the water plate, his eyes darting every which way, and hesitated at the plate's edge. Then he put his paws on it and sipped the water. The dry feathers on his tongue melted.

Benjelloun opened one eye. Charles Sebastian froze, sensing it. He lifted his head and caught her gaze. Water drops glistened on his whiskers.

She opened the other eye and held her breath, staying perfectly still.

Charles Sebastian stared back at her. His muscles strained and rippled beneath his fur, urging him to bolt. But despite that urge, he had developed positive feelings toward the girl.

After an eternity, Charles Sebastian tipped his snout to the water and drank again, sending darting glances around. He finished and skittered back to his hiding spot.

Benjelloun rubbed her sore muscles. She drank the rest of the water and lay down to sleep. "I don't know how I'm going to make it through this all alone," she whispered. Then she burst into sobs.

Unexpected Comfort

WEEKS PASSED WITH occasional rain and storms that kept the remaining sailors in the launch boat, plus one mouse and one cat, alive. We had a terrible storm that nearly sank us. The food was all but gone. I had a small stash of salted cod remaining that Special Lady couldn't reach. Despite our growing comradeship, I wasn't about to give her access to it, and she never asked me to. Once that food was gone, I wasn't sure how long she'd spare my life before she got hungry enough to eat me. I had to use the utmost care when deciding to feed her.

She noticed. Of course she did. Her tail began switching more than usual, but she remained reasonable and never stooped to begging. I hoped she understood, but we didn't discuss it.

"Perhaps we should head south," Lucía said to the captain one day. Her words had sharp points that portrayed her waning tolerance.

"I remember there's a group of islands—" Tembe said.

"Enough!" said the captain.

They tried again the next day. As the sailors bickered and grew bolder, attempting to reason with the stubborn captain, trying to get him to sail south to another group of islands that was supposedly there, Special Lady and I remained together and became . . . short-term friends, I guess. Both of us were nocturnal, and we often talked quietly at night. Once she asked, quite out of the blue, "Who is Charles Sebastian?"

I started. "How do you know his name?"

"You shouted to him the first day. And you say it in your sleep sometimes. Is he the one from the crate?"

That gave me an unsettled feeling. All this time Special Lady had kept the question to herself. "He's my brother," I said.

"The small, unappetizing-looking one? The one I chased before I ended up here?"

"Y-yes." My fur prickled. I was glad he seemed unappetizing.

"And is your mother on the ship?"

"No." I closed my eyes, pained. "No, she died. A week or two before all this happened."

"I see. Was it Marigold?" She said her name with a

sneer. "Surely not Robin—he prefers rats."

"No," I said. "It wasn't a cat. It was a rogue wave. She was out searching for fresh water . . . so. Charles Sebastian was with her. He was quite traumatized, as I'm sure you can imagine."

Special Lady bobbed her head respectfully, which I appreciated. I wasn't really sure at all that she could imagine such a thing, but it was nice she pretended to care.

"Do you really think you'll find him again?" she asked after a while. I could tell by her tone how much she doubted it, but she was at least trying to be tactful.

I looked away. I didn't want to answer that question. If I answered truthfully, I'd betray my promise. And if I lied, I'd betray my own intelligence. I'd told him I believed in him . . . but of course I didn't think I'd ever see Charles Sebastian again—not anymore. Not after all this time, all this distance traveled. But just acknowledging that made pain radiate through my bones.

There was something more to it, I realized, and it had to do with my motivation here on this agonizing journey. Without my promise to find Charles Sebastian, what did I have left to hope for? This life was terrible. Stuck in the point of a boat's bow with seawater sloshing everywhere and a *cat* as my best mate, one who could decide to eat me at any moment. There was nowhere to escape to, and she'd get me eventually if she wanted. If she tried hard enough.

That day was coming. Water was scarce, and the food was nearly gone. I would run out of crumbs soon. We were all on a nonsensical ride with a captain who'd lost his mind, aimlessly searching for an island that didn't seem to exist. No one could talk sense into him. He would be responsible for the death of everyone on this boat. Including me. And his own precious pet.

After a long while without answering Special Lady, I looked back through the slats at her. I expected she would be dozing but was surprised to see her looking straight at me, waiting to hear what I would say. She slow-blinked.

"I'm going to find my brother again," I said, resolved to believe it. "I promised. He . . . he needs me. And I need him. We're both . . . trying." My nose trembled, and a tiny squeak escaped. I didn't want her to tell me it was impossible. I didn't want anyone to speak the truth out loud. Before she could reply, I said, "How about you? Is there anyone on the ship that you miss? Or . . . love?"

The cat turned her head and gazed at the captain. She was his pet, but she hated him now after all that had happened. She wasn't loyal in the least—which was partly why

I was so worried about her relationship with me. "I miss the cook," she said with a sigh. "And his food." She hesitated. "There is another cat I was quite fond of. Robin—he's the black-and-white with a mask that makes him look like a bandit. Do you know him?"

"We've met," I said drolly. "What about Marigold?"

Special Lady's face darkened. She continued on as if I hadn't mentioned the other orange cat, as if she were some sort of rival. "The chickens were all right. We got along. I don't *miss* them, though. They're not much to chat with. Quite stupid. Never paying enough attention to the world or the conversations. They side with whoever feeds them. Do you know what I mean?"

"Um . . . ," I said, looking sideways at her. "Yes?"

The cat narrowed her eyes. And then she snuffled a laugh. "Fair enough."

I grinned, then went to sharpen my teeth on the crate. It reminded me of Charles Sebastian, the best crate-gnawer of the litter. I hoped he had something else to chew up now. It seemed to calm him.

"I really hope he's alive," I said wistfully.

Special Lady nodded. "Me too."

"And Robin."

"Thanks. I don't know why he wouldn't be."

"True." I hesitated. "Do you ever worry about death?"

"Normally? Not often. Here? Yes."

"What's that like?"

"To worry? Or not to worry?"

I looked at her. "I already know what it's like to worry."

"Right. Well, it's . . ." She paused and licked her front paw thoughtfully, then wiped it over her ears in a circular, methodical fashion. "It's carefree." She frowned and kept grooming.

I watched her, lazily intrigued by her long limbs and the way they moved. "Why don't you get along with Marigold?"

"Why does anyone not get along?" Special Lady asked. She seemed bothered by the question at first but then took it to heart. "Our personalities are very different. She's annoying. And I'm great."

I laughed. Louder than I'd laughed in ages. It felt good to expel all the stale air in my chest and suck in something fresh. Like a new start. A real friendship, almost.

"Is that it?" I asked.

The cat sighed, exasperated by my probing, and blurted out, "Marigold is my sister. I hate her."

"Oh!" I said, wide-eyed. "Sorry. That's . . . difficult." It made sense. They resembled each other. I glanced around, scrambling to find another subject to discuss. "Uh . . .

How do you suppose the anchor works?" I asked.

"What do you mean?"

"How does it keep us in place if it's just hanging there in the water beneath the boat?"

Special Lady gave me a side-eye glance. "You know there's land beneath the water, right?"

I hadn't known that. I'd thought there was land and there was water. I scrambled to make sense of it. "So the anchor rests on land beneath the water," I said slowly.

"Exactly."

"Enlightening. Thank you."

"My pleasure. Why do mice chew so much? Is it because you're nervous? It doesn't seem enjoyable."

"Chewing is essential to our survival," I told her, "because it helps us create safe hiding places. But also because our teeth never stop growing. If we didn't gnaw or chew on things to keep our teeth whittled down, they would grow so long we wouldn't be able to eat."

Special Lady seemed impressed. "If I gnawed on that wooden slat like you do, I'd have a mouthful of splinters instead of teeth."

"A toothless cat—not a bad idea."

Special Lady let out a snort like I'd never heard her make before. "Don't get your hopes up."

BY THE TIME the sun came up and I was ready for my long nap, I had developed a whole new appreciation for the feline. And she had for me as well. I hoped.

Unfortunately, that still didn't assuage my fears about what would happen when the salted cod ran out. Before we napped, I slid the last piece to her. There was no more anywhere. "This is all that's left," I said. "I'll pass the fragments to you as well." And then, because it was true, I added, "I'm sorry."

Special Lady took the bite-size piece of dried fish in her mouth like a mother mouse moving a newborn to a warmer spot in the nest. "I'll savor it," she said. And then, while I gazed at the sky, thinking about Charles Sebastian and the promises we'd made, Special Lady went to get me some water before the sailors began to stir.

A New Dilemma

TO NO ONE'S surprise, it turned out Special Lady didn't like being hungry. Our tender moments on the last night of food weren't repeated. But she didn't come after me. Not yet. Then, finally, after weeks of suffering, our stubborn captain seemed to find the land he'd been looking for. And everything changed in an instant.

Rising up with the sun behind it like some glorious goddess was Kingsland herself, an island whose people welcomed traders and didn't try to kill them. Our sailors jumped to attention, scrambling, weak as they were, to take the oar. The captain was sure this time. "It looks more developed than it was on my last visit," he said, "but I am sure this is the place."

"We're saved," one of them said like a prayer.

"To Kingsland!" cried Tembe, and the others shouted it, raising invisible mugs. The morale had gone from all-time low to all-time high. Kingsland had grown in all our minds to be a miraculous benefactor. After a journey like ours, there was no better sight on earth.

We rowed to a small flat piece of land that stretched out over the water a short distance—I admit I had a hard time understanding how it stayed in place without rolling with the waves like a boat, but it seemed solid. Perhaps it had an anchor sitting on land beneath the water. "Sails in," called the captain as we bumped against it. "Anchors down." He threw a rope with a loop on the end to a dock-hand, and he tied it to a post.

"We made it," Watson murmured, raising her hands as if the sky were responsible.

"People are coming up the pier," Tembe said. "Coming to help us. I can't wait to get off this launch boat."

I wasn't sure if I was in the clear, though. How was I going to get to safety without being trampled or eaten? I eyed Special Lady. She was licking her chops, most likely imagining the food she'd find at this lavish place, and suddenly, lacking our intimate situation in the bow and forced into this new, different element, I felt like I didn't really know her at all. Would she switch back to the cat she used to be? I blew out a breath as more and more strangers came running up the little wooden deck-over-the-sea to greet us. The sailors around me gathered their meager belongings and tried to stand up. Some were so weak they needed help.

I didn't think I could safely jump out like the others without being seen or stepped on. And I wasn't sure where I'd go once I got there. People were walking on the flat piece as if it were a ship's deck, but I couldn't see far enough to know if it actually connected to the land. Would I be stuck there with all those boots?

Then I saw a strange cat roaming the sea road, and my heart sank.

Special Lady's discerning eye was contemplating everyone's moves in an attempt to make her own. When the captain was helped out of the launch, the Lady nimbly leaped from seat to gunwale to the road, which everyone was now calling the pier. She immediately stumbled and crashed to her face, then got up as if nothing unusual had happened. Even with the bite of rations I'd fed her each day, it wasn't enough for any cat, and she looked ragged and thin. She limped along, trying to keep up with the strangers who were helping the captain. She looked back at me and stopped for a second as if waiting, but I didn't have an easy or safe way off this thing, especially with another cat in sight. Would I stumble as well? I hadn't run in ages. Could I still jump? One false move and . . .

I started to panic as I eyed my options. When Special Lady continued on after the captain, my breath caught in dismay. A great sense of abandonment overcame me. Stranger words has no mouse ever uttered: I felt so alone without the cat at my side.

As the rest of the sailors were helped out, instinct tore me in two—hide or run? In the end, I stuck to Mother's advice and hid, staying on the launch. It made sense to wait for dark, when quiet would come to this strange new world, and the roaming stranger cat would go away.

But of course, doubts found their footing and crept in. Had I lost my chance to stay with my crew? Had I lost Special Lady? What if they never returned? What if I ran out of crumbs and fresh water? I began to feel like I had made a grave mistake in waiting. Yet, I kept telling myself, I had seen no easy or safe alternative in the moment. I'd had no choice.

Where was my mother to reassure me?

When the sailors had all moved on, I ventured out, testing my legs, moving swiftly to the stern and into the space where Special Lady always disappeared to when getting water. Now I understood how rainwater had come in but seawater hadn't—there was a large crack in the transom facing in, where only rain could enter if it hit at the right angle.

There was plenty of water left in there, and I drank my

fill and took a much-needed bath besides. Then I climbed onto a bench to dry in the late sun as the wind picked up. Worried, I cast my eyes upward as waves grew and began to rock the launch and bang it against the pier. If it kept up, I'd have to time my jump just right or I'd go straight into the water. After all I'd been through, what sort of pathetic end would that be? Embarrassing.

The bustle around the launch calmed as the waves grew. Not a soul paid any attention to me. I gazed at the pier, realizing I'd need to somehow find a home close to it so I could catch wind of any discussion about ships coming or going, and keep an eye out for my sailors and the captain. With a sense of doom, I knew now that I'd made a mistake. I should have tried to tuck myself into someone's possessions when I had the chance. I should have run instead of hidden this time. I couldn't tell how big this island was, but there had been a lot of people coming and going from the pier. I feared that, along with losing the captain, I'd blown my chances of finding Charles Sebastian again. Was I stuck here?

Finally, as darkness blanketed the sea and the pier dwellers vacated, I moved to the side of the boat and waited, hoping to have a moment when the boat slammed against the pier so I could scramble across to safety without hurling myself into the water.

The world swam before my eyes. I crouched, poised for the right moment to jump, but the moment never came. Try as I might, I couldn't get myself to risk it. My weak limbs made my confidence suffer. I was stranded indefinitely, only this time I had no food to scrounge for.

I hopped down to think through my options and look for crumbs that might have landed in this part of the boat. If only the sea would calm a bit so the boat wouldn't rock quite so violently.

I happened on a few biscuit crumbs near the spot where Lucía had taken up residence. They were staler than stale, but they sufficed. As I nosed around for more, I felt—more than heard—the slightest thump. I froze and sampled the air, then slowly turned around.

There was Special Lady, inches away, glaring down at me.

Starting Again

I COULDN'T SMELL food on her breath. If Special Lady hadn't been fed, was she here to eat me? You can never, ever trust a cat. Even if you have a gentlewoman's agreement. My neighbor in captivity could be my enemy in the wild. And that's exactly what this appeared to be.

"Why are you still here?" she asked. The pier creaked, and she glanced sharply behind her, then turned back to me. "They won't be using this boat to go anywhere. I heard them talking." Her voice was soothing, but her tail swished stiffly. She took a step toward me.

I narrowed my eyes. "I couldn't make the jump once the waves picked up."

"You should have come with the captain."

"I . . . I know. I was scared. It's a risk being a mouse."

The cat seemed to ponder my fear as if she still didn't understand it, even after our talks.

"People don't worry about cats," I explained nervously, inching back against the side of the hull. I had nowhere to go without turning and bolting to my crate. "They allow you to exist among them. Let you on their laps and walk around like one of them. You're invisible if you want to be. Not so with mice. They aim to destroy us."

"True," said Special Lady. "But you're so small. You can hide anywhere."

"The fear stopped me from being able to move," I said. *As it has right now,* I wanted to add, but of course I didn't really want her to know that.

Special Lady seemed satisfied with the explanation. "Well then," she said, continuing to inch toward me with her deceiving, sweet, nimble steps, "shall I help you out of here? I don't think we're going to leave this island anytime soon."

"Hff," I said, my heart bursting from my chest. I was mesmerized by her yellow glare as she came for me, and I wondered if this was what it had been like for Olivia. Had she become frozen, too? Perhaps it hurt less that way. I closed my eyes as the cat reached me. My body trembled uncontrollably.

"There, there," soothed the monster. She lowered her evil face to me and opened her jaws. I could feel the heat of her breath on the scruff of my neck. *I'm sorry, Charles Sebastian.*

And then she had me. My nape clenched between her teeth, held like a newborn kitten. She bounded up and over the railing with my body hanging down, all my insides liquifying, my bones dripping from the skin of my limbs. The fear was so intense that I believe I fainted for a few seconds—*me*, a very brave mouse, actually fainted. But when I opened my eyes I was no longer in the cat's mouth. I was on the pier. She stared down at me.

"Is this . . . ," I whispered, trying to find my voice, "is this the part where I run and you stomp on me and it's all just a game before you devour me?"

Special Lady sat back on her haunches. She glanced all around the pier. "I'm happy to play that game if it's what you want," she said agreeably.

"And if I don't?"

"That would be my preference."

I peered up at her. "Is that . . . part of the game, too?"

Special Lady's tail switched. "Come on," she said, and she seemed . . . aggravated. Or insulted. She hopped over me and headed up the pier toward land.

I watched her go for a moment. I'd never seen this move from a cat before. She stopped and turned. "I'm not going to eat you," she called out. "But if you don't stick with me, another cat might. So *come on.*"

I followed, feeling so strange to be walking on something like this. "Everything is moving," I said as I ran in spurts along behind her. "Is this normal?"

"It's not actually moving," the cat reported. "Were you born on the ship?"

"Yes," I said.

"So this is your first time standing on solid ground. How interesting."

"It doesn't feel solid."

"It's definitely an intriguing phenomenon. You've been on a moving vessel your whole life, and you got used to the constant movement. Now that you're on land and not moving for the first time, your body senses the change, and you feel like you *are* moving."

I smiled to myself and relaxed slightly. I so enjoyed her level of discourse. What a delight.

I caught up to her and kept pace, though my limbs were burning from weeks of misuse. By the time we set foot on the island, I was out of breath and had to stop to rest. Special Lady waited for me. She was tired, too.

I lifted my head and took in the scene by moonlight and lanterns. The area to one side of the pier was a harbor with sailboats and a ship as large as the one I'd left Charles Sebastian on. To the other side, our launch and a line of other small boats were anchored or tied up. On land in front of me were structures reminiscent of the chicken coop on the ship, only much larger. Perhaps they were coops for the people, like cabins on the ship, only these were individual.

There were trees everywhere—much bigger than the oak saplings the *Carlotta* was transporting—near cabins and also concentrated not far away. And I could smell something delicious. It reminded me of the citrus in the pantry back when it had been fresh. My mouth watered.

"Ready?" Special Lady said kindly. "Pay attention to where we're going so you know how to get back to this pier. I believe that large ship in the harbor is our next ride." She pointed with her upturned nose. "When it moves, we move. Got it?"

I nodded. "Got it."

"I'll keep you informed as long as I can find you. So stay close."

Tears sprang to my eyes. I was starving. Exhausted. Overwhelmed in a strange new place. And a cat was being kind to me. "Thank you," I whispered.

She glanced at me curiously, then kept going down a

hard path near the structures and stopped in front of one that had a lovely garden in front and a tall tree. "The captain is staying here. Do you want to come inside the house with me?"

I didn't. I wanted to stay in the air. "I'll live outside in this tree," I said. "There's food here for me."

"Suit yourself. I'm sure you can figure out how to get in if you need to." Special Lady gave a little sniff, and then she headed toward the house. "Watch out for the raccoons. I've run into one tonight already. They're bold." She slipped out of sight.

"Raccoons?" I whispered, eyes wide. I had no idea what they were. "Special Lady," I called. But she was gone. For the second time in one day, I wished I'd gone after her.

Biding Time

I FOUND OUT what a raccoon was.

The smirking, rancid-smelling beast chased me up a tree. Nearly had me, too, until I found a deep knothole to squeeze into. Pushing back and flattening, I feared its claws would snag me for sure. But the hole was just tiny enough to prevent its fist from coming in far enough. It tried. For a very long time. But I was smaller than Charles Sebastian after my time at sea scrounging for crumbs, and I wasn't going to let a creepy masked creature finish me off.

Eventually it gave up and went away. I stayed in the knothole for a while, then eased out along a tree branch and dropped onto the roof of the house, discovering a way inside through a vent. Before morning I'd found a kitchen cupboard to nest in. It was filled with food, and I felt much safer inside it than out in this strange world.

When I smelled Special Lady nearby, I slipped out of the cupboard and lifted a paw. "I met a raccoon," I said in explanation.

"Wise choice," said the cat, and she moved on.

WE LIVED THERE for days. Special Lady was well fed and growing plump again after our ordeal, so I didn't feel like I was in danger. But how could I ever fully trust her? That just wasn't something mice could do with any predator. Especially their number-one enemy.

From my cupboard I listened through the crack in the door to the conversations between the captain and the couple who owned this house—they seemed to be knowledgeable about the upcoming departure of the ship that was heading to the mainland. I assumed that's where Charles Sebastian's ship would be headed, too. And somehow, someway, we'd meet up again. It kept hope alive.

When I brought it up to Special Lady, she dashed that hope to pieces.

"The *Carlotta* won't be going to the mainland," she said. "The mutineers will stay as far away as possible. They'll be hiding somewhere."

I stared and sputtered, "How do you know?"

"The captain was talking to Lucía and Tembe about it

early on. Thomas and anyone who helped him would be imprisoned or put to death if they went back home. What they did to the captain was very wrong." She studied me, as if remembering I'd had a short life. "Sending us into the launch wasn't normal. It wasn't right. That's not how humans are supposed to behave with each other. They have rules."

"Mice have rules, too. Hide instead of run. Stay together."

Special Lady shook her head. "Cats do as well, but it's different for humans. They have certain ones in charge of the rest, people who enforce the rules, and they give punishments."

"But what about Charles Sebastian?"

"He'll go with the mutineers, obviously."

"I understand that," I mumbled. But I was thrown. "If they're going off to hide, how will I find them?"

Special Lady emitted a dainty snort. But then she saw the look on my face and softened. "Clarice," she said gently, "I'm afraid there's no way. Unless you can find the ship that goes in search of them."

"Won't the captain want to do that?"

"I don't know. Not at first, anyway. He wants to return to the mainland to report the mutiny. Then someone will go after them. At least it sounds that way. Captain wants them hanged."

I'd have to go with the captain to the mainland, then somehow keep track of him there to learn when a ship would go after the mutineers? That seemed impossibly drawn out. I was a mouse—it's not like we lived forever.

The news put me in a terrible funk for days. So much so that I nearly missed our cue to leave.

Anchors Aweigh

SPECIAL LADY GRABBED me between her teeth and dropped me into a crate of supplies near the door of the house we were staying in. I burrowed down beneath something—I was too frightened to care what it was. Soon I was swinging through the air as someone carried the crate up the road. We continued down the pier, and they set me down hard. I scrambled out to look around as familiar humans gathered. My old boatmates. I didn't know where they'd been all this time, but they looked healthier. I quite liked seeing Lucía and Tembe again. They were the most compassionate of all the sailors, I thought.

The captain was there, looking almost as fit as when he'd been captain of the big ship. Tembe and Lucía moved toward him. I noticed that Lucía wore a strange expression, like something was hiding behind her eyes. She glanced at Tembe, and he nodded and stuck close beside her. My neck prickled as my fur stood on end. I didn't have a clue what was happening, but I could feel the tension like electricity in the air. I looked around for Special Lady. She'd noticed it, too, and frowned at me.

The frigate we were about to board was like an entire city to a mouse. It was so much bigger than the launch that it felt overwhelming. So huge it weighed on me. Oppressive.

Small spaces feel like freedom to a mouse. We can navigate them. With our limited vision we can take control of a space. Large spaces are absolutely terrifying. I missed the *Carlotta*'s pantry right now and wondered if Charles Sebastian was in it, missing me. I glanced at the sky between us, hoping to be calmed by its infinite presence. Oh, how I ached in that moment. Was he searching for me? Still holding his own against the ship, with all its dangers? Or had he given up on me? Had he . . . forgotten?

Part of me wished he had. The journey ahead would take me even farther from him before we could get closer. It might be too late for one or both of us.

Focusing on the current scene, I didn't like the dark and uneasy expressions of everyone around me. Something was up. When the captain stopped talking to the workers on the pier and turned to check in with the sailors from our launch, I saw Lucía step up. "Sir," she said, "I've decided to stay here. With your permission, of course."

"As have I," said Tembe. "We have no family on the mainland—no desire to go back. And your account of the mutiny is strong on its own. You have the others if you need them. With your blessing, we'd like to stay here together—"

"To inform passing ships of the missing mutineers," Lucía continued smoothly, "so that they may start looking for them. We want them found and punished. And"—she paused, then continued—"we think we can be your representatives for justice here in Kingsland."

The captain seemed taken aback. His face turned hard and stayed that way for the entire time I held my breath. I wasn't sure I understood what was happening—their intentions seemed good. But the looks they'd given each other earlier had made me think they might not be telling the full truth. Humans emanated deceit like a soft mist, but other humans rarely seemed to detect it. It was clear to me, though. And, by the look on the Lady's face, it was clear to her, too.

"I've made sure the people of Kingsland will carry out that duty," the captain argued. "Mark my words, the mutineers will be found."

"But, sir," said Lucía, who rarely called him that, "no one here has the passion that we have for finding them and bringing them their due justice. And we know what all of them look like. If we hear a whisper of them having landed and settled in some location, Tembe and I will be much closer to go after them than you will be. We won't let the sun set before we get on their trail."

Tembe added, "We'll take a crew with us that can't fail to beat them, and we'll arrest them ourselves."

The captain was still a bit thrown, and he was taking his time thinking things through. "Why did you wait until the last minute to bring this plan forward?" he demanded.

"In truth," said Lucía, "though I'm embarrassed to admit, it's because we've only just thought of it. And instinctively it felt like the smartest move, which is why we brought it to you right away. I think we could well shave the corner off the process if we're stationed in this part of the world to go after them. Catch them unawares."

Special Lady's tail began to pound the deck. I looked at her, and her eyes bored into mine. But upon my life I didn't know what she was trying to do or say. She made a soft noise and pretended to sniff at the crate. "Sneak out of the crate," she whispered.

"What?" I said. "Why?" I knew it had something to do

with what was happening here, but I didn't fully grasp it. Then I looked at the captain's face. It had cleared somewhat. He was buying the story.

"All right," said the captain. "You'll still have to testify at some point. But I suppose we have to catch them first, so there's no need for you to be present immediately. I . . . trust you. And I support this plan."

"Thank you," said Lucía. "We look forward to that day in the courtroom, staring Mr. Thomas in the eye."

"Clarice," hissed Special Lady. "Now!"

I jumped, startled. Then I slipped out between the slats.

"Run!" she whispered. "To land. To the trees."

I froze for a second, my mind trying and failing to calculate what was occurring. She jumped at me, swatting my behind toward land. "Go!"

"But—" *What about our ride to the mainland?* I turned and ran with everything I had, chased by the captain's cat up the pier. She was fast, but I was faster—perhaps that was planned as well, but I was still mystified. As the captain shouted her name, a horn sounded from the frigate.

"Special Lady!" the captain called a second time. He sounded annoyed. The captain of the new frigate was ready to set sail. Our captain, his passenger, was holding him up.

"I'll look after her," Lucía called out to him. "Don't worry, she'll be all right with me." After that, I couldn't hear anything more.

I hit land and aimed for the trees with Special Lady still hot on my tail. I hoped she wouldn't really hurt me, but I was scared enough to keep moving. Besides, things were starting to make sense, at least a little.

When I ripped up a tree and stopped on a branch, breathless and heaving, I could almost understand the attraction to running that Charles Sebastian cherished so much. I looked back and could barely make out the captain climbing into the tender that would take him to the frigate. With little argument, he'd left his cat behind. After weeks of not feeding Special Lady in the launch, she and I already knew the saddest truth.

He didn't love her.

Left Behind

"ARE YOU ALL right?" I asked Special Lady.

"Fine." She turned her back on the ship and the captain.

"Explain," I said once I could breathe again. I wasn't used to running such long stretches without looking for a tiny space to squeeze into.

"Didn't you hear them?" Special Lady said. "Lucía and Tembe. They're going to search for the mutineers."

"They didn't say that exactly," I pointed out. "They said they would do that if they heard word of them being somewhere nearby."

"Well," the cat drawled, "we know they won't go back to the mainland. So staying here with humans who will go after the mutineers puts us a lot closer to Charles Sebastian."

I stared at her, not knowing what to say. Did she truly care about that? "Pardon me—what?" I finally said.

She lifted her chin and looked away. Her tail switched, but not in a way that felt threatening to me. More like she was embarrassed. "That's what you wanted, isn't it?" she asked disdainfully.

"Of course it is!" I said. "I just . . . I'm a little . . ." I clamped my mouth shut, but then I couldn't help but add, "I'm shocked that you would go to such lengths to help me."

Special Lady didn't look at me. "I didn't want to go with him, anyway. So."

I doubted that was the reason. She would find plenty of mice to eat on that ship. But I let it stand. And as I began to piece together what had just happened and all the implications that came with it, I had even more questions.

"Do you believe that Lucía and Tembe just thought of this idea?" I asked. Special Lady had settled in a low branch of the tree to await Lucía's return. I perched on a branch above her.

"I was wary of that. They sounded like they'd concocted a somewhat complicated plan, didn't they?"

"That's what I thought, too," I said. "Something's fishy. They exchanged devious looks."

"We'll find out soon enough," said the Lady. "Here they come. Stay close behind me this time, will you? We're

149

going to get to the bottom of this together." She leaped to the ground. "I do love a good mystery."

Lucía spied Special Lady and called to her. The cat played it cool, but followed eventually.

I skittered down and around the trunk and stayed under the cover of foliage, darting from plant to plant. When the two reached the guesthouse they were staying in, they coaxed Special Lady inside, letting the door bang shut behind them. It bounced open a crack. I stayed on the porch for a moment to let them settle in, then snuck inside the sitting room and found a spot under a chest of drawers to hide. I had a perfect view of the dining nook in the next room, where Lucía and Tembe had moved into. Special Lady spread out on the cool floor between the two rooms.

Lucía sank into a chair at the table and put her head in her hands. Tembe fixed drinks and put one in front of her. "We did it," he said softly.

"Thank God," she replied, lifting her head. "One more minute with that man and I'd have killed him myself."

My eyes widened. She'd taken a lot of grief from the captain since the mutiny. And we'd known she despised him, but all this time she'd said she was loyal. Was that just for show?

"Now we need to find Thomas," said Tembe.

"If we can get our hands on a map, I think I'll be able to find him."

Did Lucía know where Mr. Thomas was going? If so, why hadn't she said anything before?

Special Lady lolled her head at me.

"Are you sure you heard him correctly?" Tembe grilled.

"He whispered it to Singh when I went to speak to him right before I got in the launch. That girl, Benjelloun, heard it, too—I saw in her eyes that she'd heard plenty. Thomas realized it, and that's why he wouldn't let her go with our boat. I wonder if she knows the power she holds over Thomas's neck." Lucía paused and frowned. "Anyway, they seized her and took her up to the prison. They didn't want her telling another soul. I fear for her— Thomas won't be kind."

My eyes widened. Heyu's half sister had been taken to the human's cage?

"True," said Tembe. "But what's this about a map? No one's been able to locate Île Obscure again since it was discovered."

"Île Obscure," Lucía said with a snort. "Perfect. We'll call it that. Better than to say the real name. Now or ever."

Tembe nodded. "The 'obscure island.' I named it myself."

Lucía swilled her drink. The liquid glowed amber in the

light from the window. "Besides," she said, "why do you think Thomas wanted to go there? Precisely because no one can find it."

Tembe let go of a deep sigh and slouched. "He's arrogant enough to believe he'll be the only one who can."

Lucía threw back the drink and slammed down her empty glass. "So am I." She pushed her chair back. "I'm going to town to look for maps and do a bit of research. I want out of here as soon as possible. After fifteen years of abuse from that man, I'm ready for a holiday."

The two of them left Special Lady and me staring at each other, mouths agape. "Did she say holiday?" I whispered once they'd gone.

"She did indeed," purred Special Lady. She stood up and arched her back in a stretch. "They're not going after the mutineers to arrest them—they're going to join them. To hide."

"And we're . . ." My jaw dropped. I didn't know the word I wanted, but I was horrified to learn of my part in all of this.

"Accomplices," said the cat with a sly grin.

A New Direction

IT TAKES ME a bit to understand how things work—like the anchor. Navigating something for the first time is not only daunting, but causes mild panic. But by now I was getting the hang of transportation, and that bolstered me. Knowing at least a little about what to expect had me sitting up inside my new crate instead of cowering all the way back to our old familiar home, the launch.

Having a friend nearby only helped things. My feline companion had grown from my worst enemy into a comfort. I had reached a state where I had to force myself to remember that she was a predator by nature. But I was now nearly convinced she would die of starvation before turning on me.

Lucía and Tembe had cleaned and repaired the launch, replacing the old tattered sail and mast and building a second one. They'd also attached a short, tented roof to the transom at the stern to provide them cover from the sun and rain. They loaded the boat with drums of water and crates of food—I clung to the inside of one of the crates, which contained fresh bananas and oranges along with something called coconuts, which were covered in hair that tickled my nose. I nibbled at the hair, finding it dry and brittle. It would make a better nest than a snack.

Listening to Lucía explain things to the islanders was fascinating. "We're going to the atolls on a hunch," she said loudly. "Mr. Thomas, who led the mutiny against our great captain, spoke the name aloud to another instigator during the takeover. In the past I'd heard him talk about Baronston Island in the atolls as a place he longed to revisit. I believe he might be hiding there."

"What about your captain?" asked one of those gathered.

"He will be well pleased if we find the mutineers," Tembe said. "If he or anyone else returns asking for us, please direct them there."

"How many mutineers are there?" asked another. "Won't they overtake you?"

"Tembe and I will be stealthy in our search. We are only looking for our ship, the *Carlotta*, and we don't intend to land. When we find it, we'll return with the information and make plans to set out with a larger group, if you are willing."

"Your captain has been our friend for many years," said the first. "We'll help you. But don't you want a larger ship?"

"We cannot afford to charter one," Lucía said modestly. "But Tembe and I have gone many leagues with this launch, and it is sturdy enough despite its small size. We don't intend to go farther than the atolls."

"That should be all right if the weather holds," said the man, sizing up the improvements they'd made to it.

With that, Lucía thanked the islanders for their hospitality, and she and Tembe got into the boat. Special Lady jumped in after them.

"Don't we want to leave the cat here?" Tembe asked Lucía quietly before they pulled the anchor and set the sails. He gave her a sharp look. "We could be searching for quite some time."

I looked up, alarmed.

Lucía glanced at the orange ball of fur and then up at the new friends on the pier who had come to bid them adieu. "Will anyone care for the captain's cat until he returns?"

"I'll take her," said one.

"No," I whispered. The blood drained from my head, and I felt woozy. I needed her. I peered out between the slats as Lucía got up and reached for the cat. But Special Lady bounded over my crate and leaped over two others, all the way to the secret hole in the transom. I saw her climb into it and disappear. I let out a breath of relief as the humans reacted with laughs.

"I guess she will be coming with us, after all," said Lucía, sitting down. "She is the captain now."

"A ship's cat through and through," said the main man on the pier. "May she bring you good luck."

Armed with so many more resources and instruments than we'd had before, we were off with Tembe at the sails and Lucía navigating. When we were far from shore, Special Lady emerged and made a point of ignoring the one who'd wanted to be rid of her. She stared disdainfully over the sea. But I could tell her feelings were hurt.

I was surprised by how much I'd come to rely on her. If she'd been sent back, would I have dared this journey alone? I didn't know the answer.

ONCE NIGHT FELL, I snuck out of the crate and found my favorite spot to hide under the triangular bow seat. It was much easier to move stealthily without many people on board. Eventually Special Lady joined me. "That was close," I whispered.

Special Lady sniffed. She wasn't over the snub. I wanted to shake my head at her, but I didn't. She finally had a taste of what it was like to be an unwanted creature. Something I'd known my whole life. It seemed a suitable lesson that she felt it for a while.

Tembe remained at the sails, and I thought Lucía was sleeping until she sat up and peered back the way we'd come. "All right," she said once it was dark. "Change course. They've seen us sail toward the atolls. We've left our proof." She blew out a breath. "Now we're free."

They were clever sailors.

We sailed in an arc, then headed for the uncharted island they'd been calling Île Obscure. My heart sang; my voice wanted to cry out: *Charles Sebastian! I am coming for you!*

But I remained silent and hoped he had stayed with the ship. What if his life and plans had changed drastically, too, and he'd found another way to come for *me*?

Survival Mode

CHARLES SEBASTIAN NESTED in the corner of the human's cage near the small hole in the wall, where he could hide if necessary. He had everything he needed, except his sister.

Sometimes, even as scared as he was, he took a walk after dark when the chickens were roosting. Not far; just to the mizzenmast to climb up and have a look around. To gather strength from its age and wisdom, and to think about how brave he had become in Clarice's absence. There was something about the mast that gave him a sense of peace as well, and it instilled a touch of comfort in his paws. While the chicken coop felt bad, the human pen felt safe, and the mizzenmast felt good. Charles Sebastian couldn't explain it more than that.

"You need a name, little guy," said Benjelloun upon Charles Sebastian's skittering return. She seemed to have resigned herself to her fate and had perked up slightly now that she was working as a sailor again.

"I have a name," Charles Sebastian squeaked. But humans were too self-absorbed to learn the language of animals, so she didn't understand. He eyed the ropes around her wrists and took a few steps toward her rather than running away.

"You're quite a fighter." Benjelloun sat back against the wall and gazed out over the cloudy sky with a troubled expression. "When the mice grow bold . . ." She didn't give Charles Sebastian a new name.

"I miss my parents," she said after a while, and she didn't cry this time. "I hope both their ships returned on the same day and they're at home together." She thought for a moment. "They wouldn't be worried about our return yet, so I'm glad about that." She sniffed the humid air. "Storm's coming."

Charles Sebastian ventured closer but stayed out of reach. He missed his mother, too.

"And Theo," she said. "I miss him, too."

Charles Sebastian wrinkled his nose. "He's a terrible person," he said, knowing she wouldn't understand.

"He didn't know what to do when my father's ship didn't arrive in time. He had this apprenticeship here on the *Carlotta*, but there was no one to care for me. I could have stayed home alone, I suppose, but I didn't want to. I begged him to let me come with him." The girl twisted her head to look at Charles Sebastian. "The upper decks are clean again now that I'm back to mopping them."

"And the chickens are fed," Charles Sebastian said. That had kept them occupied and away from him.

"I've been working on a new poem," Benjelloun said. "One that breaks my heart."

Charles Sebastian stayed still, willing her to continue, for she'd piqued his interest. "What is it?" he finally squeaked.

But she didn't recite it. Benjelloun smiled at the mouse. "You're beginning to trust me, aren't you? It's about time." She held her bound hands out to him. He could see the scabs and raw spots that never healed beneath the ropes. Mr. Thomas was a cruel and petty person. He edged closer.

Just then the food sailor came by with an armload of blankets. Charles Sebastian scurried back to his hiding place. The man tossed one of the blankets between the bars. "Storm's coming. Looks bad."

Benjelloun picked up the blanket. "I can see that. Clouds are piling on top of each other. How about letting me out of here? There must be open bunks. You can lock me in, I don't care."

"Thomas is using all the empty bunk rooms to store the saplings. Can't leave them out in the open storm," he said, sounding mildly disgusted.

"Unlike a child," said Benjelloun.

"Yes, well. You are getting another lesson, it appears."

"Who needs school when you have Mr. Thomas?" Benjelloun asked. "What did I do this time?"

The sailor shifted. "Nothing new. Mr. Thomas doesn't like you. And he thinks you're disrespectful. But most important, you know too much about his plan, and your knowing has cast a dark shadow on all of it."

"I am a *child*," Benjelloun said.

"To him, all that means is that you have a long life left— plenty of time to incriminate him."

Benjelloun grimaced and closed her eyes. After a minute she opened them and looked up at the cage's roof. It offered shade from the sun, but it wouldn't protect them much from hard rain, much less a massive storm. "This blanket isn't going to help."

"I'll take it back if you like," the sailor snapped. He rubbed his temples as if his head hurt.

Benjelloun frowned. "Can you at least unchain my ankles so I can move around beneath the roof to find the driest spots?"

The sailor glanced at the dark rolling clouds that

stretched across the sky. He swore under his breath, then unlocked the cage and came inside. "Remember I got you your job back. So don't try anything stupid, because Thomas will find out and then I'll be in here with you." He unlocked the shackles from around her ankles and slid them to where they attached to the wall. "Don't tell anybody I did that."

"Not even the judge?" she said sweetly as he hurried out and locked the pen.

"Judge?"

"In court. When you get arrested for mutiny and it comes out that you kept a child locked in a cage." She paused. "I think it would help your case."

The sailor's face went pale, and he stumbled away. I wanted to applaud, but Benjelloun's expression was even harder than before. She sniffed and pressed the blanket to her face for a long moment.

"Are you okay?" Charles Sebastian squeaked, feeling helpless.

Benjelloun removed the blanket from her face, then used it as a seat and rubbed her sore ankles. "A big storm, hmm?" she said, picking up the conversation again. She grimaced as the ropes slid over her wounds. "This is going to be interesting. And by interesting, I mean bad."

Charles Sebastian wasn't sure what to do. He'd never

been exposed to a bad storm before—he'd always had the pantry. He could sense the weight of the air decreasing, unlike the weight of fear inside him. "When I was born," he blurted out, "my mother didn't think I would survive, because I was the runt. But I did survive. And my sister Clarice—she's on the launch boat with Theo—she and I and our mother would curl up together. Little bean, big bean, and biggest bean." He paused for breath and noticed Benjelloun watching him squeak at her. "I'm the little bean," he said weakly.

"Are you *talking* to me?" Benjelloun asked, leaning toward him. She rolled onto her stomach and put her cupped hands on the deck. "Can you understand me?"

With a start, Charles Sebastian realized the girl's range had increased now that the ankle chains were gone. But for some reason, he didn't run.

"Come on, bean. You're so cute."

The mouse stared. "Did you—did you hear me talk about being the little bean?"

But the girl didn't understand him. Of course she couldn't. It had been a coincidence, though a very strong one. For a moment there he'd wondered . . . Charles Sebastian shook his head slightly and laughed. Slowly, Benjelloun pushed her hands toward him. He stepped forward, then stretched his neck and barely touched his nose to the pads of one of her fingers. Then he backed up a few steps and watched the smile light up her face. He felt it, too. A tiny bit of joy. What would Clarice think of that bravery? How he longed to tell her.

"I'll tell you my poem. It only has two lines so far." Benjelloun closed her eyes.

"I long for the moment
in which loss turns to absence."

She opened one eye. "That's it. But it feels very mature, don't you think?"

Charles Sebastian searched to define the difference between the words—*loss* was deep and cutting. *Absence*, less painful. He longed for that, too.

The first drops hit the deck and began to drum, ruining the magical moment. The wind picked up, blowing Charles Sebastian's fur the wrong way, which he despised. Without warning he became sick with longing—that intimate moment with Benjelloun had opened the floodgates of agony about Clarice. He was nowhere near absence . . . and very much stuck in loss. A whimper escaped. He fled to his hole in the back wall and started scratching and gnawing the moistening wood to make the space bigger so he could stay there as long as he needed to. And maybe Clarice could fit there, too, once he found her.

Some sailors scattered, heading below, but those

working the sails were ordered to remain in place, ready to do whatever Thomas needed to keep the ship afloat. Benjelloun watched them, then eyed the bars. Was she thinking about escape, even after she'd given her word?

Benjelloun shook her head, as if regretting her promise. She scooted all the way back, trying to get some coverage from the roof. But the rain cut sideways in sheets and slapped the deck. She huddled under her blanket, which was soon drenched. "I hope you are safe in your hole, little mouse," she called out. Charles Sebastian pressed inside the hole, able to uncurl now that he'd made it larger. He closed his eyes and imagined that the wall was his big bean. Or that he was sheltered in the palm of Benjelloun's gentle hand.

As the storm wailed and the ship careened and thudded and the forgotten prisoner cried out for help, exhaustion overtook the mouse. He plunged into sleep, only to be drowned by nightmares of running blindly through the hurricane, his eyes pecked out by chickens.

By the next day, Benjelloun was a motionless lump under the sodden blanket. Relentless rain pounded her body and rolled over the deck. Charles Sebastian—shivering and drenched, sore and stiff—desperately wished for his pantry. And barring that, his temporary haunt would suffice:

the filthy corner under the stairs. But there was no getting anywhere now without being washed away. And seemingly no hope of surviving this storm. For him or for Benjelloun or for the *Carlotta*.

In the darkest hours, Charles Sebastian realized he had never felt a sense of comradeship with a non-mouse before. But he was feeling something deep now for the pitiful lump under the blanket. Something stronger than the fear that threatened to overtake him. He hoped they both survived to share a meal again.

When the storm went quiet for a moment and the lump was still, Charles Sebastian crept across the deck and, being a somewhat-brave mouse, slipped under the blanket. He found the rope around her wrists and got to work.

The rain softened and the sky grew brighter. When Benjelloun sat up, the ropes fell off. Confused, she lifted the end of one and examined it. After a moment she glanced at the sleeping mouse in the hole in the wall. And then she put her face in her hands and laughed and laughed. "Take that, Mr. Thomas," she cried, and threw the ropes into the wind to be taken by the storm to the sea. "Take that!"

Of Nightmares Past

"TELL ME ABOUT your mother," Special Lady said. She lounged on top of my crate, and I no longer felt the need to stuff myself into a knothole.

"My mother loved the sea," I said, thinking fondly of her, with a little less aching sorrow now, which was a surprising relief. "She visited a lot of places in her two years of life, and she taught us about the world since the moment our ears could hear."

"Was she born on a ship, like you?"

"No. She was born on land, in a pile of straw shielded from the weather by a rusting, overturned bucket, not far from the docks where fishermen dumped and sorted their catch and talked about their lives." I was pleased to have remembered Mother's story so clearly. "She'd watch the ships endlessly, longing for the sea. I still don't understand it."

"Did she sneak away?" asked Special Lady.

"No, her family knew. She said goodbye and hid in a crate on the docks, then was transported onto the *Carlotta* by clinging to goods."

"Like you," the cat said.

I could picture it so much better now that I'd done it myself. With a start, I realized I'd also become something of a world traveler, just like my mother. It made me feel quite accomplished. But I still hated the sea. "And you?" I asked. "Always a ship cat?"

"No, but I was born in the captain's library on a pile of newspapers, behind a stack of dusty books. There were only two of us kittens—a small litter, the captain said."

"You and Marigold."

Special Lady grimaced.

"I still don't quite understand why you two aren't friends. Did something happen? Or have you always hated her?"

Special Lady was quiet for a long time. Then she said primly, "I don't think it's appropriate for me to say in the present company."

I blinked and looked around. "You mean me?"

"Obviously."

"Are you serious?"

Special Lady shifted uncomfortably.

"Just tell me," I urged, for I was immensely curious now.

"I don't wish to make you uncomfortable."

"Believe me," I said, "it wouldn't be the first time. You must tell me. I insist."

"Fine." She stretched, dragging this out even longer. Finally she spoke. "It's because Marigold is the best mouser on the ship."

"The best—"

"Mouser. See? I told you."

"No, no—go on," I said. "I'm fascinated." Horrified was more like it.

She glanced sideways at me. "Everyone praises her for her excellent mousing, and I'm tired of it."

My eyes widened. "Oh." I swallowed hard. "I see." And then, feebly, "But how many mice has Marigold *rescued*? I'd say you're number one in that."

"Thanks," muttered Special Lady. "But there's no reward for rescue."

"There was a reward?" I asked, horrified. "For catching the most mice?"

"Yes. The sailors placed bets on us, and Marigold won a tin of sardines. It was . . . beneath me."

"Quite," I said assuredly.

That night and every night thereafter, I brought Special Lady a reward of meat or cheese from Lucía and Tembe's stores, and we talked or sat quietly together until morning. Unfortunately our conversations were abruptly washed away by a hurricane.

TEMBE AND LUCÍA saw it coming, but there was nowhere for us to go—the storm stretched for miles across, and even with our fresh new sails, we couldn't move around it. As rain sliced and lightning and thunder struck and pounded and shook every fiber of the boat, we rolled and rocked and dropped off peaks of waves, freefalling at a heart-stopping speed. When that began, Lucía and Tembe knew we were in for it. There was no controlling the sails, so Tembe brought them in and we rode the furious sea. It owned every part of us and did as it pleased. And all four of us hung on for dear life.

My claws, which had grown back, were ripped off once more. Special Lady growled from deep inside her chest, an aching, hollow sound I'd never heard before. It haunted me. Her fur was soaked through and her ears flattened on her head, the drenching making her look more like a rat than a cat.

We all took a severe knocking; Lucía hit her head so hard that rain-diluted blood spread over her face and spattered everything around her before it got washed away. But the launch held together. Lucía and Tembe bailed and bailed until they were falling over from weariness.

Eventually we made it through to the other side. It was one of the worst experiences of my life, and I hoped my brother wasn't going through the same thing . . . wherever he was.

The night grew cold after the storm passed, and the day that followed held a chill. Tembe and Lucía collapsed under the low roof, and we floated aimlessly for a time until Lucía finally got up. She raised the sails and pointed us in the proper direction, then immediately lay down again, inert upon the bench.

Drenched and shivering, I couldn't sleep. Special Lady was miserable, too. She ventured into the weak sunshine to dry. I felt a tightness in my chest and developed a cough, and eventually fell into a restless, feverish sleep. My dreams turned to nightmares of losing Charles Sebastian all over again. Of seeing Olivia get eaten by Special Lady.

Sometime later I woke to find it dark once more. Special Lady's face was an inch away. Automatically I jump-startled, making my whole body hurt from the illness and from being banged around. I shivered and coughed.

"Are you all right?" she asked me.

"I'm afraid I'm a bit under the weather," I said with a groan. My voice was affected, and my words sounded more like a bark than a squeak.

She tiptoed her way over the items in the crate and nestled down on top of the sack that held the biscuits. "I'm dry now," she said. "I can warm you up a bit." She pointed with her nose at the curve of her belly.

I thought I might be hallucinating. Tears sprang to my eyes as an unexpected surge of emotion rolled through me. I hadn't had a good cuddle with anyone since Charles Sebastian and I were together. The thought of snuggling up to a cat was unfathomable, yet, feeling as I did, I couldn't resist the yearning. I hesitated, then snuck up through the goods and slipped into the space, pawing her fur like a newborn, sensing her heartbeat inside her warm skin. I closed my eyes.

If this illness took me, I thought, at least I'd go in comfort.

Catching a Glimpse

I LIVED.

If there was one thing I stopped doubting, it was the cat's sincerity. She was safe, and I could trust her. Special Lady and I continued our cuddle time together, and it did me a world of good. I imagine she quite liked it, too—a kind touch can be reassuring. A bit of comfort now and then; a sense of acceptance or love or sympathy. I didn't know I was craving it until it was offered, and then I couldn't get enough. My mortal enemy, Olivia's killer and devourer, a mouse's worst nightmare, had somehow, through this terrible journey, become my dearest companion.

When I was feeling better, I continued to look for the choicest morsels as gifts for her. And even though Lucía fed the cat, unlike her original owner, I was sure to top off her meal with an extra bit of dried beef or fish. And so our routine continued as we sailed to the obscure island.

Tembe and Lucía talked about meeting the ship there. I could only hope it would be so. My anticipation grew and, with it, my hope.

WE TRAVELED FOR weeks, sometimes seeing land, but not the right land. "I'll know it," Lucía assured Tembe from time to time. "On my first voyage with Thomas, fifteen years ago, we made a stop there—it was with a different captain. The place was uninhabited and stunningly beautiful. Fresh water and fruit trees. We didn't know what land it was until much later, when we discovered it had been charted incorrectly. I'm not sure if that captain ever did anything about the coordinates officially, because in Kingsland all the maps I looked at had it wrong."

"I hope no one ever fixes it," said Tembe, worried.

"One thing at a time," Lucía said. "We need to find it first."

"We're doing fine with provisions," said Tembe. "I'm just eager to take root."

"As am I," said Lucía. "Eager and paranoid. I keep looking out for ships. We appear a bit suspect in this tender out on the high sea."

"There's no reason for paranoia—we can blame the

hurricane. And just say we're searching for *them*. It's the absolute truth."

"I know." Lucía scanned the horizon anyway. "I still feel odd, though."

As time fell away and we didn't locate the island, I began to worry again that I might never see my brother. And whenever those fears and doubts popped up, I started to think of all the things that could go wrong on the ship for him. I was the heartier of the two, and I'd nearly expired multiple times.

"He could be long dead by now," I said one evening as Special Lady and I lounged together. I wanted to get used to the idea, so that if it really had happened, if Charles Sebastian hadn't lived, it wouldn't come as quite so much of a shock. "What do you know about chickens?"

"I can take them or leave them," said Special Lady.

"Did they try to peck your eyes out?"

"Mine? No. Never."

"What about a mouse's?"

Her silence worried me. Eventually she said, "I imagine Charles Sebastian would steer clear of the upper deck, which is where they stay most of the time."

Whether she was merely being kind or not, it was comforting. And I believed she was right—Charles

Sebastian would avoid the busy, open-air upper decks in favor of the darkest, quietest corner in the depths of the ship's belly. But there were so many sailors rushing around everywhere. Someone would have taken Heyu's job, in and out of the pantry all day long. Would he dare search for water without me? What if he didn't? He was such a small, frightened boy.

The memory of him cowering in the pantry while I brought him water made me nauseous. I should have made him go with me so he would know what to do. But surely he would fend for himself when there was no one left to coddle him. I had to stop dwelling on it.

Luckily, there was land.

"Do you see it?" Tembe asked. He stood up in the center of the launch, his hand shielding his eyes from the sun. "Is that the one?"

Lucía stood, too. "Hmm. It's something," she said, reaching for her maps and instruments. "We're a good sixty leagues away from where Île Obscure is charted on the map. So that could be it."

We drew closer over the course of the day. Lucía became intensely focused, trying to identify it as the island she remembered. We rounded it, and a large inlet opened up before us.

"Ooh, it's lush," Special Lady whispered, softly narrating a description of the view for my sake. "Covered with trees and brush, and a white sandy beach. Hills rise up behind the tree line, and I think I see—yes, I can hear it, too—there's a waterfall." She hopped down and then up again on one of the benches to get a better look.

"This . . . is it," said Lucía softly. Then, "This is it!"

"But there's no ship here," said Tembe, faltering.

I could see the excitement melt off Lucía's face. "Well." She was quiet for a long moment, and her shoulders deflated. "They should have been here by now. Maybe . . . maybe they've chosen a different place after all."

"Or something's gone wrong," said Tembe. "That hurricane—"

"Do you think that storm could have taken out the *Carlotta*?"

"Sounder ships have been lost in hurricanes. We were lucky to have hit the edge of it. They might not have been." They were both silent for a long while as they gazed at the island in front of them.

I could feel the warmth drain from my face. *They should have been here by now.* I looked at Special Lady. "What if the *Carlotta* arrives tomorrow? What if it's just . . . delayed?"

The cat pointed with her nose at Lucía and Tembe. "They'll think of that themselves in a moment." But even she seemed doubtful.

Would the officers choose to land or go back to Kingsland and risk missing the ship we all were searching so desperately for? I dreaded the continued journey on the sea. I dreaded more the outcome if we didn't stay and wait for the ship. But what if Tembe was right and they'd gone somewhere else? In that case I'd want to go immediately to find them.

Then Tembe said, "What do you want to do?"

Lucía's gaze swept the island, then searched Tembe's face. "This is where I want to be. At least for a little while." She took Tembe's hand. "Don't you? We could give it a try."

"Okay," said Tembe with a rare smile. "We'll give it a try."

Mixed emotions bloomed inside me. If this was where Mr. Thomas and his crew wished to meet, at least we were in a place known to them. But what if the *Carlotta* had been lost in the storm? What if they'd gone somewhere else instead? The minutes ticked by, feeling like ages, and we were none the wiser.

A New Life

LUCÍA AND TEMBE pulled the launch ashore and hooked the anchor over a fallen tree. While they unloaded, Special Lady and I snuck out of the boat to have a look around.

We didn't go far. The tree line began just off the narrow beach, and we searched slowly, methodically, looking for predators and sizing up the place. I discovered the joy of fresh berries straight away, which kept problems off my mind for the moment.

But Lucía and Tembe worried over everything, and their moods soon put me on edge. "What should we do with the launch?" Tembe asked.

"Leave it. It's too heavy to move. Besides, we need to build a shelter before dark."

"Here by the beach?"

"I think farther into the trees so it can't be seen."

"But the launch is sitting right there in the open."

Lucía gripped her hair. "Tembe," she said. "I'm just trying to get through this day, okay? We could hang for this."

"You and I haven't actually done anything wrong," Tembe reminded Lucía. "Nothing illegal. We were loyal to the captain. You set this up beautifully."

"We almost died," she reminded him. "Besides, we misled the people of Kingsland. Someone will arrive there eventually to collect us for a trial. Then they'll be out looking for us. If they find us here, lounging in the sunshine, don't you think that'll look suspicious?" She muttered under her breath. "If Thomas gets caught, he'll tell them we were in on it."

"But no one is going to find us," argued Tembe. "They think we're in the atolls."

"Thomas will tell them where we are."

"There's no way Thomas will get caught. No one even knows about the mutiny yet, except the people in Kingsland. It's too soon. They're either delayed or sunk."

I stopped listening. I had to. Their stress was radiating until they were drowning in it and vaporizing everything in their path. Besides, I had my own troubles. Special Lady could sense it. The ship was supposed to be here, and it wasn't. My brother, on that ship, potentially sunk in a hurricane. My sadness didn't need to be voiced. It was obvious that my dreams had been dashed against the rocks once more. I wasn't sure if I could take it, but I had to hold out hope that the ship would come. That it was just . . . delayed.

"Perhaps we won't stay here after all," said Special Lady. She stepped gingerly, sniffing at plants, her sharp eyes searching for anything odd or moving. "Would that be better? Or worse?"

"I'm not sure," I admitted.

A moment later, she crouched, then pounced on something long and squirmy-looking, with legs and long, thin claws, not unlike mine. She held it down with her paw and studied it. Its tail swished, and I jumped back to get away from it. Special Lady lifted her paw and the creature shot under a plant. She gave chase and pounced again.

I cringed and looked away.

IN THE END it was never my decision to stay or leave, and that almost made things easier—my fate was out of my control. When it became clear we were staying long-term, I spied a cavity in a large old tree near the shore. After scaling the tree, I found the space to be a lovely, unoccupied shelter with a nice view of the lagoon. There was a flat, uncovered space leading up to the cavity where the tree branched off three ways. The cavity itself was like a cave, big enough for me to build a nest and for Special Lady to take cover from the weather if she chose to. I only hoped she didn't bring fresh kills in with her.

In fact I was glad she'd found the little lizards to occupy her time with, because I was plunging into a funk so deep I might not see my way out. I needed some time alone with my thoughts. As I dragged soft, fibrous bits of coconut hair to my new lair, I struggled to find a way to fix this situation. I let my mind go wild, imagining chartering a tiny ship of my own, made of half a coconut shell, with a stick for a mast and a leaf for a sail. Over the waves I'd roll, sending a shout across the sea as I searched for Charles Sebastian.

Obviously I knew I could never survive it. But I realized in that moment that I'd made it my entire life's goal to reunite with my brother. And without the ability to do that, what was the point of anything? Why build a nest? Why search for dewdrops on leaves or tasty roots and seeds and berries or broken coconut shells for a nibble? Why do anything at all? Did Charles Sebastian feel the same way? Helpless? Unable to control anything? Had he changed, like I had? Adapted to his situation? I hoped so, but doubts lingered. What if he'd been attacked moments after we last spoke, and I was wasting all my time and risking my life to find someone who wasn't there?

Special Lady waited for me at the base of the tree as I scurried down for more nesting materials. "You can go up and take a look, if you like," I said. "I found a spot large enough for both of us."

The cat didn't go. Instead she studied me. "Are you going to be okay?" she asked.

I dug at the ground. I didn't know the answer. All I knew was that I needed something. Maybe it was a nest, but I doubted it. Maybe it was fresh water. Or food. But that wasn't filling me right now, no matter how much I ate. "I'm trying," I said after a while, and bit into some more coconut-shell hair. I spit the prize on the ground to start a pile. "It's hard to explain what it's like to lose your whole family."

Special Lady tilted her head quizzically as she looked at me. I took in a sharp breath—of course she was alone, too. How could I be so selfish?

That night, while Tembe and Lucía slept under a scant lean-to they'd built, Special Lady and I roamed the beach and the forest. We visited the spot where the waterfall

landed and had a refreshing drink. From a smooth stone nearby, I could feel the impact of that hard, deadly water reverberate in my chest, trying to rattle something awake inside me.

But all was dormant.

Later, when Special Lady went to look for something to eat, I sat out on the beach in the shadow of a boulder and stared upward. "There's only this one sky between us," I pleaded. "That's all. That's it."

But it was a very big sky.

Rekindling

AS IT HAPPENS with mice, I grew thick, and then I grew thin again. The food was plentiful but tasteless to someone who'd lost all hope. Separation from my brother would be permanent, and I had to accept it, but I couldn't. In the swell of desperation, I'd made a promise, and I'd held hope in his return promise. I'd said I believed, and I'd desperately wanted to. But now, in the dullness of safety, I was helpless to fulfill my end, and it left me empty. Would he be disappointed in me for not doing more? But what was *he* doing on *his* end of the sea? Was he trying? If I knew my brother, he'd have given up long before now.

I chided myself for thinking like that. Perhaps I didn't know my brother.

Special Lady tolerated my moods for a while. Then she gave me space.

Perhaps that was what I needed to work through this.

I wanted to ask more about her family. Was her mother

still alive? Did she have a tale of hope to offer me? But what if she didn't? I couldn't find the heart to hear another sad story. So I didn't ask.

Special Lady roamed the island but visited me from time to time to check in and give me a cuddle. I think that's what kept me going, but I have little recollection of feeling much of anything for a while. Sometimes I sat in my tree for days and Special Lady brought me drops of water on her whiskers, like old times. She was a gem, being kind to me when I couldn't do the same for her.

Other times I snapped out of my self-absorption and looked around my new home. The island had lizards and turtles that left me alone. Birds, as well, and I had to keep an eye out for the larger ones. But for the most part, if I kept to the trees, I was safe.

Lucía and Tembe had brought flint, seeds, nets, and traps from Kingsland. Their lean-to, set far back from the beach, grew into a shelter that kept out the occasional squall. As time passed, they began to build more earnestly. Logs became planks, planks became walls, walls became a house structure not unlike those we saw in Kingsland. They were settling here. *We* were.

The more days that went by, the more worried and anxious Lucía became. But then at some point, her worry abated. Perhaps there was a magical number of days that had to pass in order for humans to free themselves of guilt. I had no idea, but they appeared to have reached the threshold. The air around them lightened, and somehow that helped with my mood as well.

They planted a garden with seeds they'd brought from Kingsland, which turned out to be the delight of my new life here. There was something about the fragile sprouts first poking up from the earth, all wrinkled and newborn, that renewed an inkling of hope in me. If not for reuniting with Charles Sebastian, then perhaps finding another mouse companion somewhere on this island. No one would take the place of my brother. But I was a social creature, and I'd lived months of my life without another mouse in sight.

Truth be told, I missed the closeness with Special Lady. Being in the garden made me realize so many things like that, and it became a meditation spot for me.

One breezy morning, I found the cat lying on the path that had been formed by Tembe's and Lucía's trips back and forth to the beach. Special Lady watched the lizards sun themselves but was too lazy or bored to go after any of them. I kept to the side of the path out of habit, even though the boots walking it were few and far between. "Hello," I said, feeling awkward.

Special Lady did that thing she does to humans—

ignored me completely. I would have to put some work in to earn back her attention, and I was ready to do so.

"I noticed an especially fat lizard on the rocks near the waterfall," I offered. "Feasting on flies." I glanced sideways at her. "Looking a bit arrogant."

She switched her tail.

"There are some nice herbs coming up in the garden already," I said, "in case you get an upset stomach. I noticed you were nibbling on grass the other day. I could bring you some when they're ready."

Special Lady rolled onto her back, paws in the air, bent at the wrists.

"Do you want me to give you a scritch?" I asked, coming out from under the plant. I glanced around nervously for large birds, then began working my paws over the cat's belly. She started to purr, and I breathed a quiet sigh of relief.

When I heard a footfall on the path, I bolted under some leaves. "What's that now?" said Tembe. "Did you see that?"

"See what?" asked Lucía.

"I must be losing my eyesight. I could have sworn the cat was getting her belly rubbed by a mouse."

Lucía snorted. "You have lost it." They continued to the beach.

Special Lady rolled over and got to her feet, then started nosing around in the leaves. "Are you still here?"

"Yes." I came out from hiding. "That was a close call."

"They wouldn't have done anything. You're a mouse in the wild now. It's different. People are territorial if you're in their personal homes or boats, stealing their food. Out here . . ." She sort of shrugged her shoulders. "You're safer. From *them*, anyway."

"What do you mean?"

"Just beware of the birds."

"I know." I was mildly annoyed that she didn't assume I was aware of this already, but I wasn't about to argue.

"Especially, I mean," the cat emphasized. "I saw a large bird take off with a mouse in its beak last evening. I . . . thought it might have gotten you."

"Well." I blinked. Her frankness rattled me, and I rushed too quickly to cover up my unease with a joke. "Did you feel bad about it?"

Her eyes flickered. "Of course I did. What do you think?" She scowled for having to admit it. "I had to go check your tree to find out."

I was moved. "Oh," I said, the word forming a lump in my throat. I looked up with a rush of sincerity. "Thank you. I will be vigilant. And I'm sorry I've been so down. I'm trying to feel better. I *am* feeling . . . better."

As I said it, I realized it was true. "I'm going to be okay."

Something Big

I SETTLED DOWN near Special Lady and replayed our conversation in my mind. "So, you said there was another mouse?"

The Lady cast a sly look my way. "Well . . . not anymore."

I gulped. "Fair enough. Have you seen others?"

"I had a chase the other day. They're not like you. Bigger, coarser fur, with a longer tail. More like a small rat."

"Oh." The edge of my mouth curled. I didn't warm to the sound of that.

"Might have been the same one that the bird got, though. It was down on the other side of the inlet."

"Oh," I said again. Far away. If I could have my wishes granted, I'd want everything I ever needed right together or just a short distance from one another. Food, water, nest. Everything was safer that way.

I didn't want my spirits to sink, so instead I focused

on my renewed friendship with Special Lady. "If you find any smallish mice near my tree, would you let me know?"

The cat grinned saucily, and her tail curled up and over her back. "I can't let *all* the mice go, now, can I? What kind of cat would I be if I started introducing mice to each other?" She paused. "Besides, there might be a contest."

"What!" I exclaimed before I realized she was joking. Once my wits returned, I remembered what I'd wanted to ask her. "I've been meaning to inquire: Is your mother still living in the captain's house on the mainland?"

She seemed taken aback by the question and gazed out over the path. "I don't know. I haven't seen her since I was very small. I've been on three voyages with the captain. None of them nearly as remarkable as this one."

"Marigold too?"

"Yes, unfortunately we've been together our entire lives. Until recently." She didn't seem sad about that.

"Do you miss her? Maybe just a little?"

"I suppose. I miss Robin more. He's very funny."

"Any . . . kittens?"

"Oh." She stiffened. "Yes, of course. I don't know where they are. You understand ships." She clamped her mouth shut, and I knew she didn't want to talk about that anymore.

"You've been such a good friend to me," I said quietly.

She closed her eyes and didn't answer.

Just then a shout rang out from the beach. Seconds later, Tembe came sprinting past, heading for the house, startling both me and the cat this time.

"Where are you going?" Lucía called out.

"To get the spyglass!"

Lucía came running up the path as well. "Do you think it's him?" she called.

Special Lady turned sharply, then sprinted up a tree to get a better look. I stayed hidden in the brush. What was going on? Who was "him"? Had the captain arrived in search of these two? And what did that mean for me? For us? Were we about to be on the move again?

"What do you see?" I squeaked up at Special Lady.

"Nothing," she said. She stayed there, straining her neck, searching. I climbed up to be with her, though I knew that if she couldn't see anything, there was no chance I would be able to. Soon the humans came down the path again. They raced to the beach and stopped. Lucía put the spyglass to her eye and gazed out.

"Is it the captain?" asked Tembe, his voice anxious.

"I'm not . . . ," said Lucía. She adjusted the spyglass and wiped the lens, then put it back to her eye.

"Can you see the ensign?" Tembe prompted impatiently.

After a moment, she slowly lowered the glass and looked at him, her face unreadable. "The flag is in tatters. But I'm sure it's the *Carlotta* coming our way at last."

Anticipation

I BELIEVE I fainted for a moment before roaring to life.

Our old ship. She was limping into the inlet as we stared, looking much worse for wear. It seemed too good to be true. Doubt sparred with uncontrollable hope. Could my brother be there?

"They're going to think the captain is here when they see the launch," said Lucía, panic in her voice. "Come, Tembe. We have to go meet them so they know it's only us." They shoved the launch into the water and ran with it, then climbed in and grabbed the oars.

Special Lady and I got down from the tree and paced the end of the path near the beach. "I'm not sure how . . . ," the cat muttered. "Think!"

Clearly something was on her mind, though I didn't ask what—I was still processing. But a huge question surfaced right away: If the *Carlotta* dropped anchor, how would we get Charles Sebastian here? That was followed immediately by the ever-present and more ominous question: Was Charles Sebastian still alive? After all this time, I wasn't sure I was ready for the answer.

"Charles Sebastian!" I screeched, hopping up and down on the path. "Charles Sebastian!"

"Save your voice for when they're closer," Special Lady snapped.

She was right. I reined in my instincts to call out again.

WE COULDN'T TELL what was happening with the launch or whether Lucía and Tembe's journey to the ship was successful. But eventually, finally, the ship seemed to be coming closer.

"They're dropping the anchor," Special Lady said after a time. "The launch is pulled up alongside. Come on. Let's get as close as we can." We moved down to the shoreline, where the sand was hard-soaked and easier to stand on.

"Charles Sebastian!" I yelled. "Charles Sebastian!"

There was no answer.

"They're loading the launch with supplies," Special Lady reported. "Now they're lowering the other tender. Some of the sailors are coming down the cargo nets and into the tenders."

"Charles Sebastian!" I was desperate for an answer. Desperate to believe in the declaration I'd made. Then it struck me: Had my mother felt this way after she'd said it to me? Had she expected me to prove her right just for saying it? I closed my eyes, trying to sort that out. Then I extended up on my back feet. "Charles Sebastian!" My voice flew backward in the wind, and the words slapped my face.

"They're coming," Special Lady announced. "And there are more people still on the ship. That means they'll take another trip in the smaller boats. Tell your brother! Tell him to stow away on the supplies. Tell him to jump into the jolly boat when it returns."

I screamed it all, but I still hadn't heard a peep from him. There was little chance he could hear me, anyway, with the wind our enemy.

The launch arrived first, anchoring offshore, then the smaller tender. Several sailors I recognized climbed out and sloshed ashore, carrying goods. "Climb onto my back," Special Lady ordered me. "We're going into the small tender. Dig deep into my fur. Don't let go!"

I squawked. I couldn't see a way that it would work, and that uncertainty glued my feet to the sand. "We'll drown!" I said.

"I'll go by myself, then. Stay safe." As the boat ebbed

and flowed with the waves near the shore, she approached the water as if she were stepping on quicksand.

"Wait!" I stared at her. "What are you doing?"

"I'm going to get your brother."

"But—"

"Quiet now." She leaped into the oncoming wave and paddled to the jolly with a look of disgust on her face, barely keeping her rat-face above the surface.

I darted out of the way as sailors emptied onto the beach. One of them grabbed Special Lady out of the water and tossed her to the shore. She landed on all fours, snarling, and ran back into the water, determined to get into the tender. When she reached it, the remaining sailor picked her up out of the water. He stood up. "Smith!" he called. "Take this blasted cat out of here. I'm going back for the next load."

The man named Smith splashed through the water to the jolly and took the cat. Special Lady fought him, but he held her tight to his chest. "She seems determined to get back to the ship," he said with an uneasy laugh.

"Maybe she thinks the captain is there," said the man in the boat.

"No idea why she'd want to be anywhere near that monster," said Smith.

"Keep her away." The man in the tender started rowing

back to the *Carlotta*. Special Lady finally managed to twist out of Smith's hands, scratching him in the process. He dropped her, uttering an oath, then kicked her in the side before she could bound away. She screeched and bowled over and sprang to her feet, then sprinted to the tree line to nurse her wounds.

I ran over the loose sand to be near her while she fumed.

"Go back to the shore, idiot!" she said, her face and body distorting in pain. "Tell your brother to hide in the crates. It's his only way off the ship."

Her sharp words stung, but I did as she said. As hope drained into the sand, I screamed again and again and again for my brother, until my squeak was no more than air and a vibration.

Charles Sebastian didn't answer.

The launch and the jolly boat made several trips until nightfall, when finally all the sailors and the goods and supplies and chickens and cats that they could catch were onshore.

Charles Sebastian, if he was among the goods, was mute. But I knew better. He'd be screaming for me, too.

Which meant he wasn't there at all.

Despair

THE MUTINOUS LEADER, Mr. Thomas, was the last to step onshore. Lucía greeted him with an icy glare. "Where've you been?"

"We had to make a stop," he said. She waited, arms crossed, and he continued. "We dropped off several sailors in the atolls. The ones who'd wanted to go with the captain and you but couldn't fit." He paused, then added, "It was better that way—they were a whinging lot."

"Do they know you were planning to come here?"

"Of course not, Lucía. What do you take me for?"

"Well, good. What about the girl who overheard?"

"We kept her away from the others."

Lucía's eyebrow raised. "How?"

Mr. Thomas glanced away with a guilty look. "It doesn't matter. She's here now."

Lucía stared daggers at him. "I need to see the girl. Immediately."

"Why? She's fine."

"She needs to know her half brother is dead."

Thomas blanched. "Oh."

Lucía turned sharply and called the man to come with her, leaving me absorbing that part of the story. The girl. Heyu's half sister. She was here. And she was about to get the news I was dreading to get for myself.

.

I STAYED ON the beach as darkness came, waiting for the wind to die down and the calm that sometimes came with night.

But the clouds rolled overhead and the wind and waves picked up, and I was nearly swept to sea as the tide came in. Soon the rain started, and I was forced back to my shelter.

Wet and covered in sand, I dodged the sailors who were trying to take cover in the downpour. Then I shivered in my nest until Special Lady appeared. She licked me clean like I was one of her kits, then warmed me in the curve of her belly. "I'm sorry," she said quietly. "You're not an idiot."

"I know," I said, but her saying it made me feel better. Both of us were injured—her externally, me internally. The storm made everything worse. But without Special Lady, I might not have survived the night.

It rained and blew torrentially for two nights. The sailors were miserable, and without shelters on the island, many of them went back to the ship to hunker down in their cabins until the storm passed. Special Lady and I stayed in the hollow, getting drenched as the trees were soaked through and the wind whipped everything around. We swayed and silently begged for it to end, dozing in between bouts. At least we weren't on the sea.

Finally, at dawn, the world quieted. By the time we woke, the sailors were coming back from the *Carlotta*. I jumped to my feet. The wind was dead, and moisture hung like an invisible pelt on our shoulders.

I ran down the tree and around the puddles to the shore, steering well clear of the sailors and keeping an eye out for birds on the prowl. "Charles Sebastian," I called. "Charles Sebastian!"

I heard no response but the racket of men and women eager to start life over. "Charles Sebastian," I cried again as a gull swooped down and snatched a sodden moth trying to fly. I bolted to safety. No doubt the birds were as hungry as I was after the deluge. I snuck back to my tree.

"Any response?" Special Lady asked. She licked the storm remnants from her fur. Bits of bark and sand were everywhere, and she smelled of the steamy earth.

"No."

"Any food?"

I gave her a look.

"That was a joke." She got up and stretched, one back leg straight out at a time. Then she left to go in search of food for herself.

I had one of those moments where I felt like everything was a bit too real and seemed wrong. Like, here I was, living in a tree, lost in paradise, with my best friend, a cat.

And my brother was gone.

Hope

SPECIAL LADY FOUND Robin. He and Marigold had been brought ashore and were getting used to life on land. Special Lady disappeared for a few hours, and I worried I'd lost her for good now that she had her friend back. But I was happy for her and tried not to feel bad about it. Eventually she returned to our tree and settled in around dusk to watch the sunset.

"How is Robin?" I said, trying to sound like I cared about cats other than her.

"Lovely," she said. "He told me they put Benjelloun in the human's cage and left her there, even through the hurricane."

I was horrified. "All because she overheard Thomas?"

"I imagine so. You see? Strange human punishments."

"How did she survive that?"

"I forgot to ask."

"Did you speak with Marigold, too?" I asked.

"Briefly," said the Lady, glancing at me.

"And?"

"I suppose it was nice to see her. I . . . I feel lucky." She gave me a sorrowful look that made me tear up. She was thinking of me.

I left it at that, for the next moment we saw a young girl walk down the path, making her way to the beach. It had to be Benjelloun, Heyu's half sister, who was supposed to have come with us.

She was crying.

THAT NIGHT, WHEN all was calm and dry, I returned to the beach and stared at the blurry mass of a ship in the water. My birthplace: the *Carlotta*. I glanced at the launch boat and imagined pushing it into the water and drifting over to the big ship, then climbing up the ropes and searching the entire place to find out if Charles Sebastian truly was not there. How would I know for sure otherwise? I needed to learn what had happened to him, but I felt achingly certain I never would. His story felt unfinished, cut short before the climax, and that made me more sad than anything. It couldn't be over.

In the quiet, I wanted with all my heart to believe he

had soldiered through it all. He was smart. The best gnawer I'd ever known. He'd use those teeth to build a shelter. He'd go after water when no one else did it for him. He'd stay safe . . . for my sake. Because I asked him to.

I let out a shuddering breath, then chose to believe in him, without a single doubt. I rose up and called out one last time, my voice breaking: "Charles Sebastian! It only takes one mouse to believe in you! And that one mouse is me!"

I waited as the words soared and echoed against the sea and bounced off the ship. "Charles Sebastian," I sobbed. "It only takes one mouse to believe in you! And that one mouse"—I choked on the words—"is me."

A bird stirred in a nearby tree and settled again.

And then.

"Clarice!"

A New Dilemma

I COULDN'T BELIEVE my ears. Was I hallucinating? Was my grief tricking me? "Charles Sebastian!"

"Clarice!"

"You're alive!"

"*You're* alive!"

"We did it!" I hopped on the sand. "We did it!"

Charles Sebastian was silent for a moment, and then he called out, "How do I get across the sea to you?"

I stopped hopping. How indeed?

Before I could answer, I heard a low yowl that made my limbs shake. A cat's paw slapped me down and held me there, my neck wrenched and my face pressed into the hard-packed sand. The feline's breath, its teeth coming around me. I squealed. The cat let me up and pressed down again before I could bolt. I knew this game. Do I play dead? Try to run, only to be stopped? All the hope and excitement I'd gained a minute ago drained out of me. Was it really going to end like this?

A second later, something plowed into the offender, knocking it down and sending me rolling across the shore. A slow wave crept under me and nudged me toward the sea.

I got up, dazed, and tried to shake the cobwebs out so I could remember which way to flee. Then Special Lady jumped at me and grabbed me in her teeth. She ran for our tree, with me dangling unceremoniously. I looked back and saw Marigold skulking. The storm had made me forget about the new residents.

"Clarice?" I heard faintly from the ship.

"Stay safe!" I shrieked. "I'll be back!"

"Pleethe thtop thcreaming," said Special Lady. She paused at the base of our tree, then climbed. Once inside the hollow, she set me down. "You're lucky I was there." She looked hard at me. "Now Marigold will think I'm greedy or vindictive, stealing her mouse. She'll hold a grudge for a long time."

"Isn't that what cats do for fun?" I muttered, checking myself over. My neck was sore, but Marigold's teeth hadn't pierced it. Then I looked up. "He's alive. We talked!"

"I know." Special Lady softened. "I'm glad. That's why I

was right there—I was coming because I heard you yelling to him."

"I—" I looked at her, finally comprehending what she'd done for me just now. I blew out a breath. "I could have been eaten a mere moment after finding my brother." I felt dizzy as I imagined the tragedy of that. Looking back at her, I gave her my heart. "Thank you."

Her whiskers twitched, and she pretended to look outside the tree for Marigold. "You must be vigilant," she said. "I've asked Robin to leave you alone, but that doesn't mean he'll do it. And I can't save you every time from the other one."

"I will be careful," I said quietly. "I'm sorry. I lost my head when I heard Charles Sebastian's voice."

She gave a stiff, single nod. Then she settled into place like a toadstool, legs drawn in beneath her, and closed her eyes. I knew she didn't want to talk about it. Feelings embarrassed her.

I crept under the overhang of her fur for warmth and comfort and once again imagined sailing the launch to fetch my brother. Even if it magically got loose from the sand, I had no way to steer it. I was desperate to reach Charles Sebastian, but I had an ounce of sense. And if Charles Sebastian had made it this long, he had gained some common sense, too. Or perhaps he'd had it all along and the rest of us had smothered it before he could show it to us.

Marigold had given me an important reminder. One false move and there would be no reunion. And all of this would have been for nothing.

Nemesis

CHARLES SEBASTIAN HAD thought he was the only one left. But his squeaks to Clarice alerted the other remaining resident on the ship—the attack chicken, who'd somehow managed to escape the lunging grabs of sailors as they disembarked with all their belongings. The bird hadn't been cared for in days and had resorted to roaming the lower decks, looking for crumbs. Hungry.

That could be bad news for a small mouse.

CHARLES SEBASTIAN HAD the entire upper deck to himself. The human's cage was empty now—back when the ship had stopped moving and the rain had passed, two sailors had finally come for Benjelloun. They unlocked the cage and yanked her out of it, not even noticing or caring that the prisoner's wrists were free. She'd looked back. "Wait!" she said. She seemed flustered, like she wanted to go back for her belongings, but she had none. "Just hold on a moment!" She'd tried to wrench free.

"No time!" said one of the sailors, not letting go of her arm. "The last tender is waiting on us. Your sentence is over. You're free. Unless you want us to leave you here." The girl bit her lip, eyes searching the wall. Then she turned and stumbled along with the sailors, out of sight.

Charles Sebastian had stared back at her from his little hole. He'd run out, then run back inside again, unsure what to do. "Benjelloun," he'd squeaked, but the sailors had been so rough, he feared he'd be squashed.

He knew she'd been looking back for him. How he wished he'd dared to go with his friend. In the flurry of activity, he should have hopped onto her shirttails or the top of her boot. But by the time the sailors were there for her, it had been too late to make such a risky move. And besides, how would Benjelloun react to him jumping on her? She might bat him away, as people did to mice—even mice they liked, he supposed. But who could ever imagine a mouse so bold as to go along with a human, who could crush it in its hand? No mouse Charles Sebastian knew. In the end it was too frightening. And that was that.

* * *

HE REGRETTED IT now. *Especially* now. Because Clarice was on the island.

How had she done it? How had she survived? How had she gotten away from the captain and found the right people to travel with? It was a marvel to Charles Sebastian.

But now that they had found each other, they'd have to figure out a way to be together. She was right there! A shout away. The joy in his heart was so great that it exploded through his fur and rained down on the deck like the hurricane they'd come through. He had found her!

There was a bit more to do.

To celebrate the joyous night, the tremendous freedom, the incredible discovery of Clarice, Charles Sebastian ran in circles and up and down the empty deck. He did a backflip, then dashed to the mizzenmast and hopped up, clinging to it while his eyes darted frantically. Then he climbed all the way to the top and looked toward land. He saw bursts of fuzzy firelight slipping down paths. The shadow line of trees against the darkening sky. Clarice was just there. Just there! "Clarice," he called again, though she'd told him she'd be back later. Had enough time gone by?

After gazing toward the island for some time from the top of the mast, Charles Sebastian's excitement began to deflate. How . . . ? He dared not think about it. Clarice was the pragmatic one—she'd said so herself a million times. She'd find a way.

Charles Sebastian eased down the mast and nearly headed toward his home in the human's cage. But he didn't have any food or water there now that Benjelloun had left. Perhaps, with everyone gone, he could find the pantry. There would be water in the kitchen. With a start, he realized how normal his plans seemed, compared with months ago. He could find the pantry, and it sounded like an adventure.

He headed to the nearest steps and started quickly down them into the dark beneath. Before his eyes could fully adjust, he ran into something . . . feathery.

The chicken squawked in surprise. Charles Sebastian panicked. He ran, slamming into a post, then scrambled to his feet and went around it when he should have gone up it. The hungry chicken chased after him, half flying, half running, across the entire length of the ship. Over the lower decks they scuttled, twisting and turning through passageways and down another flight of stairs. Running into things in the pitch darkness.

"Clarice!" Charles Sebastian screamed. But she didn't answer. He needed to think. Where was the mizzenmast?

He'd be safe there. But the mast was in the sunlight, and they were nowhere near that. With a burst of speed, the mouse flew down one more staircase. He landed at the bottom before the chicken started down. Instead of tearing through the hallway, Charles Sebastian made an unexpected turn and found himself under the stairs. In the filthy corner where he'd hidden once before.

The tired chicken continued after him slowly, not giving up. Charles Sebastian crouched. He remembered his time here before, vowing to haunt the space beneath the steps. Was this how it all would end, just out of reach of his sister? Death by chicken?

Charles Sebastian flattened. He touched his ragged ear with one paw, gathering strength and courage and anger from it. This chicken had done that to him. He thought of all the things he'd accomplished without realizing it—surviving cats and chickens and boots on his own. Making friends with a human, and even freeing her wrists from rope. As the fowl reached the deck and hesitated, unsure of where to find the mouse, Charles Sebastian waited. One moment. Two.

The chicken clucked and took a few steps toward him. He stayed still, willing his heart to quiet down for fear of it being heard. When the chicken continued, Charles

Sebastian felt a strange low growl coming from inside him—a noise he never knew he could make. Taking strength from it, he leaped from his corner, front paws outstretched, jaw opened wide, teeth bared. With a mighty, mousey roar, he landed on the chicken's neck and sank his claws in. Then he bit down hard on the flapping wattle and hung there, sinking his teeth in deep.

The chicken squawked and fluttered and clucked and flapped uproariously, trying to loosen the attacker's grip.

But Charles Sebastian bit down and held on for his life, swinging wildly from one side of the chicken's neck to the other, grasping feathers and pulling with all his might.

The chicken flopped to its side and clawed at the mouse. Charles Sebastian let out a bloodcurdling screech of pain. He released his bite. "You will never forget me," Charles Sebastian snarled, then bit down in a new place even harder and continued to squeak, "And you will never bother me again!" He shook the wattle, then let go and rebounded off the chicken's side. He tore back up the flights of ladders and across the deck in a race to safety, where the lingering essence of prisoner Benjelloun would rise up like a spirit and praise him for the fine work he'd done. He'd paid the chicken back for both of them.

How he wished she were still here so he could tell her.

* * *

AS THE ADRENALINE wore off, he dozed, dreaming of Clarice and telling her how brave he'd been. And in the dream, she said she knew he had it in him all this time. It gave him a brand-new feeling of peace . . . like he just might make it after all.

Something Unsettling

SAILORS MOVED AROUND the island by day, cutting down trees, building homes, cooking meals over fires, and talking about their futures. They all carried an amount of uneasiness with them—it permeated their clothing and filled the air, and it left me looking over my shoulder constantly, as if they were forecasting the next horrible event. Who knew what it would be?

Special Lady and I, and sometimes Robin, snuck around together, listening to them in the evenings as they discussed making Île Obscure their permanent home.

"Tell me exactly what you said to the people in Kingsland," Thomas asked Lucía and Tembe.

"I've already told you," Tembe said gruffly. His back was stiff as a board, and waves of disgust emanated from him when it came to Mr. Thomas. They might have wanted the same thing—mutiny—but they weren't friends over it.

Special Lady and I speculated about Thomas having been the one to administer the stripes on Tembe's chest before the mutiny . . . perhaps to make it appear they weren't in cahoots.

Lucía looked Mr. Thomas squarely in the eye. "We told them we heard a rumor that the mutineers were heading to the atolls, and that we were going in search of the ship. If we found it, we'd return and get assistance from our dear friends in Kingsland." She paused for a measured breath. "We told them that if the captain returned before us, they should let him know where we were."

"And you're sure they didn't see you head in the opposite direction?"

"Yes. Positive. Now stop with the interrogation. We are partners, not your underlings." Lucía stood up, and she was a full mouse taller than Mr. Thomas. He shrank back and ended the line of questioning.

Lucía went on to address the mutineers. "I believe this island is the best place for us—it's incorrectly charted and difficult to find. The climate is perfect, and the food and water are plentiful." She hesitated. "Could the captain find us? I imagine he could. But that chance is possible anywhere on earth."

"So what's the real question?" asked a sailor.

"The real question is, what if a ship happens by and sees the *Carlotta*?"

The group erupted in noise, and we slunk away.

THERE WAS ONLY the girl who seemed resigned to whatever fate came her way: Benjelloun. We'd watched her brother die, yet we could do little for her. Special Lady made an effort to allow the girl to pet her, which she did with fervor. Her aura was of one who cared about animals—we can always tell. And at one moment upon her arrival, I thought I could almost smell Charles Sebastian on her clothing. It was wishful thinking, no doubt. He wouldn't have gone anywhere near the human's cage, out in the open.

The girl was calmer, but sadder than the others, too. Lucía had invited her into her home, but soon the girl had built her own shelter, away from the rest. I wasn't sure why Benjelloun caught my interest so forcefully, considering how much I'd despised her half brother. But she seemed special. Shiny, like no other human I'd known.

CHARLES SEBASTIAN AND I shouted back and forth every night for the next week while Special Lady watched my back.

"If anyone returns to the ship, you must hitch a ride back with them," I shouted to him.

"I'll try," he said.

I glanced at Special Lady.

"Tell him about the gangplank and the cargo net," Special Lady prompted. I was grateful for her help, for she knew so much more about the ship itself than I did.

"You can squeeze through the gangplank door," I told him. "Or climb down the cargo net and jump into the launch from there!" Any way possible that he could see. "Are you scared? Because I know you can do this!"

"I'm a little scared," he said, which made my heart sink. "But I fought a chicken, Clarice."

I was afraid I hadn't heard him correctly. "You fought a chicken?"

"Yes! I bit it in the wattle and growled! It won't be bothering me anymore."

Special Lady gurgled with laughter. "You're worried about *him*?"

I felt a surge of confidence about his abilities, but I wanted to be sure everything went without a hitch from this point forward. "Stay in listening range," I coached him. "Learn the ship so you can go to the ropes in an instant. Educate yourself, like Mother taught us! You'll run out of water and food soon. You must take the first chance!"

"I'll do my best," he said.

Did he comprehend the seriousness of this? He'd never been anywhere but that ship. He absolutely had to take the next opportunity, no matter what it was. He couldn't let his impulses take over. My throat ached from yelling, and my nerves were frazzled with worry. He was so close, yet impossible to reach.

When Special Lady and I retreated to our tree after that discourse with Charles Sebastian, she only stayed a moment before leaving me alone to brood. "Something's in the air," she said, sounding troubled. "I'm going to listen in on Lucía and Tembe. They're having a meeting soon with the entire crew. I'll let you know what I find out."

I was too tired to go with her.

A moment later, she was padding up the path to the cabins, making the chickens jump and flutter on their way to roost. I plugged a small hole with my body inside the large tree cavity and waited, trying to disperse my anxiety into the wood around me and send it to the outmost twigs to drop away like dead leaves. Trying to dwell on the happiness of getting another chance to speak with Charles Sebastian. Instinct, perseverance, luck, and a friendship with a cat had led me here, where Charles Sebastian came to arrive. It was more than a coincidence. It was our mother's words that had shaped things for me. She believed in me. Period. It didn't matter what I'd done with those words—whether they'd caused me to doubt myself more or less.

And when I'd said them to Charles Sebastian, it had not obligated him to change in any way. The words were mine alone, and I either believed in him or I didn't. *It only takes one mouse,* Mother had said. The emphasis was on the believer, not the believed. Did the words also inspire the believed?

For me, they had.

Her declaration of belief in me had led me to believe in myself. To trust myself. To have the tenacity to threaten a cat and become her food peddler. To make key moves when the stakes were sky high, like running down an endless pier being chased by a cat when I thought I should have hidden in a crate and gone with the captain again. It had been the opposite of Mother's advice. But I'd had the courage to make that choice.

Perhaps Mother had known her end was near, or that it could be. Perhaps she knew that Charles Sebastian and I would need to lean on each other someday. To believe in each other. I was grateful for her words.

But screaming them over the sea to my brother was not enough.

As the night wore on, I dozed, and when I woke, Special Lady still hadn't returned. The sun was coming up, and though I couldn't see the sunrise yet, I could tell the sky was growing lighter. I heard a familiar scratching pattern on the bark; it was Special Lady.

"Clarice, wake up." She said it with an urgency I wasn't used to.

"I'm awake," I said, spiraling in the hole and crawling out. "What's wrong?"

Before she could tell me, I could hear a few sailors starting down the path. "I'll explain in a minute. We have to go. Now!"

I gasped as she nabbed me at the back of my neck. She scrambled down the tree and jumped to the ground, rattling my brain, and ran toward the beach faster than I'd ever known her to run. So fast, my eyeballs jiggled.

The jolly boat was pulled halfway onto the beach, and the launch was anchored in the water a short distance offshore. Special Lady bounded onto the jolly and ran the length of it, then jumped. We arced and hit the water with a shocking splash. Before I could take a breath, I was plunged under, and all sounds were instantly muted. Seconds later, she pulled me above the surface, still in her mouth. She was swimming, and though she tried to hold me high, I was bobbing in and out of the water. I tried to gasp for breath at the right times, but everything about this was disorienting, and I ended up choking and coughing and gasping for air.

A moment later, we were climbing up the side of the launch. Special Lady reached for the anchor chain to pull herself up. Soon her head crested the gunwale, and she dropped me into the boat. I coughed and wheezed and dragged in a choppy breath as she pulled herself in. "What do you think you're doing?" I demanded between gasps. "You almost killed me!"

"I almost killed myself," said Special Lady. "Quick— hide so they don't throw us overboard." She went to her spot and disappeared in the transom. I hesitated, looking at my favorite familiar place in the bow, but without a crate there to shield me, it didn't feel safe. Instead, I followed Special Lady so we could be together. I needed to find out what was going on.

"Please explain," I said, crawling up. A small pool of water sloshed on the other side of a support piece from where we crouched, remnants of the recent rainstorm. I could hear two voices getting closer and sailors pushing through the shallow water toward us.

Special Lady's ears twitched. She didn't answer at first, and her hesitation made fear grip my heart.

"What's happening?" I whispered.

By the sounds of it, the two sailors dropped heavy containers into the boat. The sudden swaying meant they were climbing in.

The cat ducked her head through the hole and narrowed her eyes, studying the scene.

"Special Lady?" I prompted.

She lifted her head and turned toward me as we rocked back and forth. "I need you to stay calm when I tell you this."

The serious look on her face was one I'll never forget. "Okay," I said. "I will. I promise."

She dipped her head, then said gravely, "They're going to torch the ship."

Removing All Traces

"WHAT?" I ASKED, incredulous. "You mean burn it? Right now?"

"Yes." Special Lady caught herself as we were jostled about once more. Finally the two sailors were in place, and as one pulled up the anchor, the other picked up an oar.

"Why?" It seemed irrational. And horrifying, considering the obvious issue that was squeezing my heart.

"Because if the captain or any other search parties sail past here, they'll see the ship and know this is where the mutineers are hiding. They have to destroy it."

"But then . . . they'll never be able to leave this island." The concept was less concrete than what I was used to. But I was more worried about Charles Sebastian. I looked up. "How are we going to save my brother? What are the containers for?" I wrinkled up my nose—the smell wafting in our direction was vaguely familiar and intense enough to make my head buzz.

"I don't know exactly," said Special Lady. "But they are going to set the ship on fire. When they go aboard, you must immediately tell Charles Sebastian to come down the cargo nets and jump into this boat. We'll guide him. Do you think he can do that?"

"He'll have to." He'd survived this long without me, after all. But there were nets all around the ship. He'd have to find the right ones.

"You'll talk him through it."

I shot Special Lady a grateful look. She was going way beyond what any friend would do. I never expected that feeding her all those months ago would result in anything more than not being eaten.

We drifted up to the side of the ship, and I was antsy for the sailors to leave so I could emerge from the transom and talk to Charles Sebastian. The sailors secured the launch, then took the containers and climbed up the ship's nets, over the railing and onto the lower deck. As soon as they were climbing, I emerged and called to my brother.

"Charles Sebastian! We're here in the launch. Port side of the bow. Climb over the railing and come down to us in the boat." I waited anxiously to hear him respond.

When he didn't, I shouted the same instructions again.

"I'm coming!" Charles Sebastian called back this time. "Trying, anyway."

Special Lady jumped down from the hole, then up onto the bench seat, and perched with her front feet on the gunwale. She peered upward, looking for movement on the railing.

"Charles Sebastian!" I cried again, growing desperate. Where was he? "Go to the lower deck. Port side! Bow!"

"I'm here! But there's no way to climb up to the railing from where I am," Charles Sebastian called. "It's sheer wall, too slick. I have to find a place where I can get traction."

The cargo nets were hung from the lower deck railing and came to rest a short distance above the launch. I moved cautiously toward the lowest rung of rope, measuring the distance with my eyes.

"What are you doing?" asked Special Lady, alarmed.

"I'm going after him," I said. "If there's a fire, he won't know what to do. He'll panic."

"Clarice," Special Lady said. "He's made it this long without you. Have a little faith."

"There's no time for that." I climbed onto the gunwale next to Special Lady and waited until we drifted close to the ship. Then I took a deep breath and jumped for the net, digging into it with my claws, and pulled myself up.

"I'm coming with you." Special Lady waited until I scrambled all the way up the net and was safely on the deck before following so she wouldn't shake the ropes and throw me off.

She landed behind me as I called for Charles Sebastian again. "I'm here! On the lower deck near the anchor. Where *are* you?" My frustration was growing.

"Clarice!" came his voice, but I couldn't locate him. "I'm here, but I smell a cat!"

"It's Special Lady. She's safe to be around, I promise. Come out. We have to *hurry*!"

"Are you sure?" he asked, his voice faltering. "She ate our sister!" Did he doubt everything now? Including his own ears? I would have if I were him.

"Do you think I should go back to the boat?" Special Lady whispered.

"No. We might need your help." I turned back to the direction Charles Sebastian's voice had come from. "Listen to me. They're going to burn the ship," I said, trying to sound calm but not doing a very good job of it. "We must escape right now. The cat is my friend. I know it sounds . . . impossible. She won't hurt you, I promise. She's quite something. She has, in fact, risked her life for you." It was such a pure truth that it choked me up. The cat had more than repaid me, and she continued to do so, with no expectation of anything in return.

Charles Sebastian poked his nose up from behind a coil of rope, and I spotted him. *Finally.* I rushed over as boots pounded above our heads and the smell of what was in those containers choked us. *Kerosene.* I recognized it now that it was burning. Smoke drifted toward us.

Charles Sebastian and I touched noses. We embraced. "Charles Sebastian," I whispered.

"Clarice," he said, his voice cracking.

We cried for a moment. But there wasn't time for anything else right now. "Come with me," I said. "You must. Now that we're together, we must stay together, always. It's going to be okay."

My brother was quaking, yet he somehow found the gumption to proceed. "The chicken," he said. "It's around here. Prowling. Angry at me."

He seemed delirious. I noticed his ear was split and ragged, and guessed he'd had a run-in with one of the other ship's cats—a chicken couldn't possibly do that, could it? "Whatever it was, you survived it," I said. "You're strong. You can do this."

"I know," he said.

I turned to Special Lady. "Will you please tell my brother that you won't hurt him?"

Special Lady seemed startled, but she immediately recovered. "Upon my life, I will not harm you," she said with utmost sincerity, and I felt a warmth no mouse has ever felt for a cat before.

"All right," said Charles Sebastian.

And that was that. Charles Sebastian came after me. We moved in fits and starts and found a rough patch of wall we could climb all the way to the railing and over to the cargo net. Smoke filled the air. The acrid stench was sudden and almost overpowering. The ship was massively on fire. Boots pounded toward us. I turned to Special Lady in alarm.

"They're coming," she whispered.

"Go!" I said to her. "Get to your hiding place in the launch."

She hesitated. "I can take one of you with me."

We heard a crash as one of the flaming masts toppled and hit the water, missing us by mere feet. It sizzled and smoked and bobbed on the sea. The brittle wood of the ship was swiftly catching fire.

I glanced at Charles Sebastian, trying to come up with a scenario that wouldn't put him into further distress. But I didn't trust him to come down on his own if Special Lady took me, and I didn't want him to be traumatized by going in the jaws of a cat. "It won't work. Go!" I urged the cat again. "The sailors are here. We'll go right behind them so they don't send us flying. They won't see us."

She understood and jumped to the net, then made her way down and into the boat. Charles Sebastian and I crouched in the shadow of the ornately carved railing, which would soon be destroyed. The men headed down the net, carrying flaming torches. We heard more crashing from the upper deck and saw the first flames licking the stairs from belowdecks—they'd lit the ship everywhere. The air was increasingly thick with smoke. "Come," I said. "Stay calm. Don't run."

"I'm okay, Clarice. Really."

Special Lady screeched a warning. I looked down and saw one of the sailors untying the launch. The other was holding his torch to the bottom of the net. He was setting *it* on fire, too! Panicking, I jumped to the top of the net and screamed for Charles Sebastian to follow. Something switched in my mind, turning this from a rescue mission to a survival mission. In that moment, I did something unspeakable. Something I would regret for a very long time, for it affected more than just myself. It affected the two creatures I loved more than anything.

I abandoned my brother and jumped for my life.

Abandon Ship

I HIT THE water, unbeknownst to the men, and it took my breath away. Special Lady had scrapped her plan to hide and saw me leap. I plunged under, deeper than I'd ever been before. Then I floated to the surface and sucked in a breath of smoke, then choked on that and water together. There was no worse feeling I'd ever experienced. But I was numb with fear, and my feet paddled automatically as the waves lifted and lowered me at their callous whim.

I couldn't think, couldn't process anything. I just paddled, trying to stay afloat as my limbs grew tired. I bumped into something and automatically turned toward it, desperate to hold on to anything that would save me. It was a piece of the scorched, fallen foremast. I hoisted my sodden, heavy body on top of it and collapsed. When I'd caught my breath and regained some sense, I turned sharply. Where was Charles Sebastian? Had he jumped behind me? Or was he still on the doomed ship, succumbing to smoke?

I saw movement on the burning net, then heard the sailors raise their voices and point. Special Lady charged through the flames and climbed the burning net to the top. The sailors shouted her name, shocked to see her. She stopped at the gunwale, and though I couldn't see her clearly, I thought she grabbed Charles Sebastian in her mouth.

The net was engulfed in flames now—there was no going back for the cat. Without hesitation, she jumped away from the fire, toward me, and landed with a splash. I watched, my heart in my throat. Would she surface? Did she have my brother?

An endless amount of time passed, and then her rat-like head emerged. I always forgot how small she was beneath the orange fluff, but she looked even smaller now against the vastness of the ocean and the backdrop of the enormous ship on fire. She lifted her chin, and I saw a gray lump of fur in her mouth. She had him.

She swam toward me, struggling. Fighting the waves. Fighting the current. Fighting to breathe through the smoke. I tried to paddle the mast toward her, but my tiny paws had no effect on anything. She slipped under a wave, then came up again. Pushing. Struggling to stay alive with every ounce of strength to keep Charles Sebastian safe.

The men lost sight of her in the sea of debris and abandoned her for dead. They rowed with great strokes toward shore as the ship cracked and moaned. Flaming charcoal bits hit and sizzled in the water all around me, and I watched Special Lady go under again.

"No!" I screamed, my voice ragged. "Special Lady! Don't give up! Don't leave me!"

She resurfaced. Charles Sebastian was limp and unmoving in the grips of her jaws.

"You're almost here!" I encouraged.

Special Lady continued. I could detect her front paws treading just under the surface. I could see Charles Sebastian barely above the water. His eyes were closed. The fact that I'd abandoned him left me numb. And I'd put Special Lady in danger at the same time. How could I have done that? I'd never forgive myself.

Finally Special Lady reached my mast. My lifeboat. She dropped Charles Sebastian onto it and fell away, struggling in the water, not wanting to put her weight on the end of the broken mast for fear of dipping us into the sea and losing us all over again.

Our eyes met. Frantic. In desperation, I said the only words that came to mind. "It only takes one mouse to believe in you, and that one mouse is me!"

She chittered pitifully, but couldn't stay afloat without sinking us.

"I believe in you," I whispered. And I meant it with all my heart.

Seconds later, the mizzenmast fell, striking the sea behind her. She slipped under the water and disappeared.

One Last Chance

"NO!" I SQUEALED. I stood tall, peering at the spot Special Lady had gone under, but she didn't resurface. "No!" I cried again, my voice ragged. This couldn't be happening! But she was gone, and there was no way I could save her. And Charles Sebastian was here, unconscious. I crawled along the mast to Charles Sebastian and called his name. I took him by the nape of the neck and dragged him to the thick end of the mast, which allowed for the widest berth and the least amount of water washing over. I could feel my lungs rejecting the smoke that hung above us and all around. Was Charles Sebastian alive? After all that Special Lady had done, after giving her life, had it been worth anything?

I was benumbed.

"Charles Sebastian," I hissed, trying to sound commanding, as if that would wake him from death more easily than a gentle plea. I pressed into him. Opened his mouth and blew into it. Pushed his chest. Did everything I'd witnessed Lucía do to Heyu after he'd nearly drowned.

I had no idea what would bring Charles Sebastian back to me, but I was willing to try anything. Finally I curled around him, like old times. Like in our pantry crate with the coffee and flour. Big bean and little bean. Missing our biggest bean. But her words lived inside me.

As we floated, I retold the stories of when we were young: Mother teaching us about the world and her travels. Showing us the ship life. Telling us it was okay to use big words even if we weren't sure what they meant. I recalled our deep chats about what mutiny was. And I reminded him of our promises to find each other again. "We did," I said, my voice faltering. "We did find each other, Charles Sebastian. And I'm so sorry I left you on the cargo net. Please, you *must* live so that we can enjoy our lives together." He didn't move. "Please," I said again.

The image of Special Lady's soaked rat-face appeared uninvited in my mind. I'd let her down, too. I'd caused this catastrophe by losing my head and jumping. She'd rushed to right my wrong. If I'd waited for Charles Sebastian, if we'd jumped together, would Special Lady still be alive? Safe in the launch?

After a while, I looked up. I didn't know where we were or what direction we were heading. Out to sea? To the shore? It didn't matter. Nothing mattered.

I squished against my brother, willing my heartbeat to startle his. Willing my stare to cause his eyes to open. "Charles Sebastian," I whispered. "Please come back."

When we bumped against the crow's nest, floating flat and free from its mast, I dragged my brother onto it and prayed it would eventually find the shore. Exhausted, I curled around Charles Sebastian again and let shock take over. There was nothing more I could do. For him, or for anyone.

An Empty Space

WE FLOATED AMONG a forest of scorched oak saplings.

The sun baked us dry, and I spread my body over Charles Sebastian's to protect him. He wasn't stiff, which I thought meant he was still alive, though his eyes hadn't opened. I couldn't let myself think he was dead—it was more than this mouse could take for the moment. I also couldn't let my mind wander to Special Lady without it causing me to fall apart. I loved her.

I would shout it from the top of the waterfall if I ever found land again. I loved a cat, and she had loved me, too. Her last act was so surprising, so unlike everything we'd been taught, that I could scarcely believe it. And I knew then that if I ever made it to shore alive, and if I were ever to have a family, I would tell them the tales of the most amazing cat, Special Lady, who'd eaten one of my siblings for sport and died saving another.

I could hardly bear breathing because of the heavy, jagged pieces of my heart stabbing my lungs. Perhaps, like Charles Sebastian, they were waterlogged, for the combined bits felt heavier than the rest of my body.

Thirsty, delirious, baking on blackened wood with my pink tail burning, I fell into a fevered sleep.

WE WASHED UP against the shore in the middle of the night, and even then, I wasn't sure what to do. The crow's nest had become our new home and, as always, it was frightening to venture away in the open air. I wouldn't be able to drag my brother very far. When I bit into Charles Sebastian's skin to pull him, he jumped and squealed in pain.

"Charles Sebastian," I demanded, dragging him to the sand. "Fight against the darkness! Open your eyes!"

He flopped. After a moment, he did as I said. "Clarice," he croaked. "Clarice, I'm here."

It did me in. After everything that had happened—nearly drowning, burning, choking, dying—that's when I finally broke. I broke from hearing him say my name. And from knowing that I'd never hear Special Lady say it again. I closed my eyes and swallowed, dry air scraping my swollen throat. "Steel up," I whispered. "We have to keep moving."

We sat in a damp hollow of sand and watched the moon cross the sky together. Once Charles Sebastian regained some of his strength, we went to the cover of trees and found drops of morning dew and something to eat. I wasn't sure where my tree home was, though I had a sense of which direction to travel in. I realized it didn't really matter where we settled now. The thought choked me up.

My life was a series of trade-offs. When I lost Charles Sebastian, I found Special Lady. And the second I found my brother, I lost my best friend. Why couldn't I have them both, even for a little while? "Why is everything so hard?" I whispered.

Charles Sebastian rested his chin on my back. "I don't know."

IT'S NOT IN a mouse's nature to travel. My experiences were not typical. A normal mouse born in a ship's pantry would live their few years calling that pantry home forever and stray only a short distance from it. Charles Sebastian wasn't conditioned for this—trudging through the plants and trees of a rocky island. He'd never experienced the world outside a ship before. Nor had he walked on such uneven ground with sticks and insects and birds to watch

out for. He was overwhelmed and exhausted. Barely hanging on. Our steps were agonizingly slow. We didn't get far.

"The ground is moving," he remarked.

"It only feels that way," I told him. And then I started
crying.

Eventually we found a rotten log to burrow into and
curled up and spent the day there, sleeping. Cuddling.
Comforting each other. Tasting insects for the first time.

We told stories of the time in-between. He told me
about his survival experience with the ship cats and
chicken attacks and the prisoner girl. He described her,
and I told him I'd seen her. Benjelloun, the solitary one.

"She's okay? At the camp?"

"Yes," I said. Then, "Heyu is dead."

"Oh," he said. "Oh no."

Then I told him my story . . . some of it, anyway. Part
of me wanted to share about Special Lady. About how we
became friends over time. About how we were not just
friends, but something more than that. Something deeper
and more lasting, more unselfish than most friendships
could ever be.

But I couldn't find the words.

My mind battled itself. The one I'd doubted was here
with me, and the one I'd truly believed in was gone. Joy

and sorrow pushed each other down and pulled each other up like frightened mates. I was elated to have my brother curled up with me again. And devastated to have lost my best companion. Charles Sebastian would never comprehend my love for the cat. So I mourned the words that didn't exist to express that, too.

In the end, to protect my heart, I skimmed over the story of Special Lady, telling Charles Sebastian that it had been an arrangement based on need, and leaving it cold like that for now. Though I reassured him that the cat would never have eaten him. I told him that she had saved his life as a gift to me.

He had no memory of her kindness. Another shot to the heart.

When night fell, we set out again along the edge of the woods, keeping the sea in sight. I didn't know where I was going, but I knew we had to go this way, and our trek became a pilgrimage to the spot where Special Lady had last walked the earth . . . and a quest for Charles Sebastian to find Benjelloun to see if she was okay. My heart grew heavier and heavier as the shock of everything wore off. I couldn't get the picture out of my head: Special Lady's face slipping under the surface. I knew how much she despised being wet. Yet she hadn't hesitated. She'd joined my cause without question. Without me even asking. We'd become something special, like her name.

I paused to rest as the moonlight reflected on a tree and caught my eye. A drop of sap came out of the tree, like a tear. Even the trees were mourning. I reached up and picked the tear, then turned to feed the sweetness to my brother.

"I remembered the words you called out from the launch," Charles Sebastian said as we continued walking.

"Which ones?"

" 'It only takes one mouse to believe in you, and that one mouse is me,' " he said. "Why did you say that to me? I've been thinking about it."

"Mother said it to me right before she died. Did she not tell you as well?"

"No."

"I'm sure she intended to," I said. "That's why she took you with her to get water."

"I thought you were telling it to me because you and Mother and the rest always believed me to be helpless. And you wanted to give me courage." He stopped. "Did you really believe in me? Or did you doubt that I'd survive more than a few days?"

I looked down, feeling awful. Then I lifted my chin

and turned to him. "Of course I believed in you." After a pause, I added, "You *were* pretty helpless, though."

"Why not, when everyone doted on me?" He laughed softly. "Being alone so suddenly and tragically—it was the hardest thing, Clarice."

"Yes, it was."

We trudged onward.

"How did you cope?" he asked.

I was quiet for a while, thinking of the ways. "I looked at the sky," I said. "And I knew it connected us. There was only the sky between us, and it made the world feel smaller."

"Hmm," said Charles Sebastian, and it came out like a musical note. "I quite like that."

"Did you believe we'd find each other?"

"Of course I did," said Charles Sebastian. I knew he was lying, too, but it was the right answer. "I love you," he added.

"I love you, too." My eyes stung.

WE STUMBLED INTO camp. Wearily, as dawn broke, I led my brother to my tree and invited him up. And as we curled up together in a space too vast for two mice without a cat, I noticed a tuft of Special Lady's fur that had snagged on a sharp edge of bark. And I knew that was why I needed to return here, despite the sailors. I needed this fur.

While Charles Sebastian gazed out over the land from our perch, I weaved the strands of Special Lady's fur into our coconut-husk nest. As I worked, I imagined Special Lady was just out walking, or eavesdropping on the sailors, or chasing lizards. "There's only the sky between us," I choked, my chest caving in.

"Only the sky between," agreed Charles Sebastian sleepily. In seconds, he was in the nest, falling asleep.

And I was falling apart.

Only the Sky Between

WHEN WE AWOKE, the *Carlotta* was gone; all the charred pieces had either washed ashore or sunk. Several of the sailors pulled the launch out of the water and brought it up the path to store deep in the trees, out of sight. They hid the smaller tender there as well and brought it out only now and again to fish with. My brother and I were happy to have zero boats or ships in our lives, and we kept away from the ocean.

Robin came by, looking for Special Lady, and I had to tell him the sad news. Then, as we traveled the path in search of Charles Sebastian's friend, Marigold appeared, uninvited and unwelcome. We bounded up the nearest tree, but the melon-colored ruffian didn't try to harm us. "Robin found me," she said. "Can you tell me what happened, please?" She tried to act aloof, but I could see she was shaken.

I told her everything. Marigold thanked me stiffly and went away.

The next day, Charles Sebastian and I finally happened across the path of Benjelloun. I stayed off to the side, under the cover of plants. But Charles Sebastian darted straight toward her and hopped. Then he stopped and stared up at her; a bold and brazen move. I was afraid for him until she knelt in the path. "I can't believe this," she murmured, and looked closer. "You are a resourceful little mousie, aren't you? How on earth did you get here? I've been thinking about you ever since they dragged me out of prison." She held her hand out to him. "My wrists are healed," she said, pointing to the discolored skin. "Thanks to you."

My curiosity was piqued. What was she talking about?

"Your ear makes you look very tough," she said as he approached and touched her fingertip with his nose. Her eyes filled. "My half brother is dead."

Charles Sebastian stayed by the girl, unafraid.

After that, Benjelloun began to leave berries on the edge of the path for him. He led her to our tree once, and she often stopped nearby to see if he would come out. When he did, she'd settle on the path and tell him stories and recite poetry, as if that were normal. I didn't quite grasp the dynamics of their relationship, but I envied it now that I'd lost my own unusual friend.

I remained heartbroken.

I wanted to heal, but my heart wasn't ready. Perhaps, as it happens with mice, I would forget Special Lady in time. But I hadn't forgotten Charles Sebastian, and he hadn't forgotten me. I cherished every second with him. He grew stronger, and we went everywhere together. I would not lose him again.

I taught my brother to be watchful of birds, and he told me that albatrosses are lucky. I explained that the lizards and turtles were not interested in us, so they were safe, and he explained how to take a chicken down by the wattle. I showed him how to find dew on the leaves in the morning before we went to sleep, and where the best berries grew, and how to dig under logs for tasty insects. And he taught me that Benjelloun would feed us if we ever lacked for anything. He'd managed to play the runt card with a human. And it worked. Not that I was complaining.

We slept the days away, with one ear pointed toward the opening of the tree's cavity. The cats left us alone—Robin, who continued to abide by his promise, and Marigold, perhaps out of respect. We would have plenty of warning if they changed their mind, though, for the scratch of a cat's claws on bark was instantly recognizable. And we trusted no cat, ever. Not anymore.

Charles Sebastian gnawed out the little hole that I'd used as a hiding place before, making it big enough for both of us if a predator came. We tried it nightly when the cats howled and fought and made us uneasy. Their snarls sounded too close for comfort whenever darkness and calm fell over the island. Every note was clear as a bell in the night.

I longed for my friend. I dreamed she was alive over and over again, only to wake and relive the moment when she'd disappeared. Sometimes, when a cat howl startled me awake, I'd call out, confused: "Special Lady?"

Charles Sebastian seemed worried about me. To assuage his fear, I slowly told him the real, complicated story of Special Lady and me. Yes, I said, she ate Olivia. Yes, I said, she saved our lives. I told him how I'd fed her, and how we'd struck a deal to keep her from eating me. I told him how she'd brought me water droplets on her whiskers, and how we'd learned about where the *Carlotta* might be heading. How we'd stowed away on the launch a second time to go in search of him. How Special Lady had heard about the sailors going to torch the ship with him on it, and how she'd grabbed me and risked everything so we could get to him.

I started to cry, and then I couldn't stop. Charles Sebastian tried to console me, but there was nothing he could do. My friend was gone, and with her, my heart.

IT WAS AFTER we fell asleep that the dreaded scratching came to our tree. Both of us jumped backward in alarm and immediately scrambled into the safety hole. I peered out and listened. Was it Marigold or Robin? Charles Sebastian's heart pounded in time with mine. If the cats decided they were done being nice, we might have to leave for a new home, because they'd never give up.

We waited as the animal's scratching continued, getting closer. Louder. It had to be Marigold. When a dirty, scrawny cat's face appeared, backlit by the sun, I squinted, not recognizing it.

The cat looked around the empty hollow, and her tired eyes turned wet and sorrowful. She hung there, not coming in or going back down, for a long moment. "Clarice," she whispered. "I believed in you."

One Day by the Sea

I GASPED. THIS scrawny, dirty cat was *my* scrawny, dirty cat. "Special Lady?" I whispered, poking my nose out of the hiding hole. "Is it really you?"

She turned and caught sight of me. We stared at each other for an infinite second. And then I jumped out and ran to her. She struggled and pulled herself into the tree cavity, then touched her nose to mine. She looked a wreck, with scratches and dried blood and burns and missing patches of fur. She collapsed in the hollow. "You're alive," she whispered, like she'd lost her voice.

"*You're* alive!" I said, overcome. I couldn't silence my cries. I started cleaning the caked mud from her face. She lay still, not purring. Not moving. But breathing. She was definitely breathing. I turned to see Charles Sebastian peering out of the hiding hole. "Come," I said to him. "Let's get her some water."

We went out and found a curled leaf filled with dew.

We carried it between us, climbing the tree ever so slowly and carefully so we wouldn't spill, and left it for Special Lady to lap up. Then we went after food, going straight to the camp. I dove recklessly into their stores, finding the best fish I could come up with. I passed a hunk to Charles Sebastian and took some myself, and we stumbled, top heavy, back to our tree and set our gifts next to the leaf. The water was gone—a good sign. We would find more. As much as it took to keep Special Lady alive.

I STAYED BY my cat's side and nursed her back to health. Charles Sebastian, though mildly fearful at having a cat in our living quarters, never questioned what we were doing and never wavered when we were out on a mission to find food or water. He trusted me. He believed in me. And I in him.

When Special Lady felt better, she told us what had happened. "After I went under, I resurfaced and found more of the ship's wreckage floating nearby, big enough to hold me. By the time I was safely balanced on some, I couldn't see you anymore. But I heard you, Clarice. Your voice rang in my ears. You believed in me. You knew I could survive. And I wasn't going to let you down."

I felt a lump grow in my throat.

The cat paused. "I got caught in a current, though,

and went out to sea instead of toward the shore—a most disheartening and disturbing feeling. The waves took me around the island and farther away, and always, every moment, I tried to pay attention to where I was. But I never got close enough to shore to swim for it. I thought I was doomed. When one of those large fishing birds started circling overhead, I really believed I was done for. It came at me and scooped me up."

"The horror," I murmured, eyes wide. "What did you do?"

"I fought it at first but soon realized if it dropped me, I'd land in the sea without a piece of wood to float on, which would be the end of me. It headed for the island, and when it soared low, about to land, I gave it the fight of my life. We tussled and hit the ground. I clawed and bit and fought with every ounce of energy I had left. And then, when it finally let go, I ran for the woods."

"You poor thing," I said. "No wonder you were in such a bad way."

"What happened next?" asked Charles Sebastian. He was riveted.

"I started my trek to find you. I walked for days, hardly stopping to sleep or eat. Your words were a chant in my head, Clarice. I knew you believed in me. I was going to survive. And I had to find you."

"Did you believe we had survived the sea?"

"After all you did to find your brother," Special Lady said, "I'd hoped there could be no other option. You would survive—or at least I needed to believe that. When I finally made it back and poked my head up here and didn't see you, I was devastated. I couldn't bear the thought that you hadn't returned."

I dropped my gaze. I didn't want to tell her that I had believed she was dead. I didn't want her to know I had doubted her. I'd doubted Charles Sebastian, too, many times. Perhaps I needed to say my mother's words again, and believe them this time.

ONE FINE DAY, while we three were sleeping in our tree—little bean, big bean, and biggest bean—a flurry of activity on the main path woke us. Lucía and Tembe were there, and Thomas and the rest, even Benjelloun. They stopped short of going to the beach. Lucía carried the spyglass and held it to her eye.

A ship was coming. The sailors' language grew salty and colorful. All day they took turns watching, melted against trees for cover. We listened in with half an ear to their constant, nervous speculation. Was it just a random ship? Or was it the captain, searching for the mutineers?

Would they suspect them to be hiding here? Would they all be captured and taken back to the mainland to be hanged?

"I hope it's Benjelloun's parents, coming to find her at last," Charles Sebastian said. "Though I would miss her terribly."

Special Lady glanced sideways at him. "If it's the captain, he'll be sure to take special care of Benjelloun on this journey, I can assure you," she said dryly. "She'll be a star witness. And she'll go back to her parents if they've been found."

"And what shall we do?" I asked, feeling my chest tighten. "Is this our home now? Or are we destined for ship life?"

"I shall stay with you, Clarice," Charles Sebastian said. "Whatever you decide. But I quite like it here. I never understood Mother's love for the sea."

I felt a rush of relief, but I tried not to show it. I wanted everyone's true feelings out in front of us. I looked at the cat. "And you, m'lady? You're a ship's cat. Do you wish to revisit your life's work as second-best mouser?"

Special Lady watched as Marigold chased down the path toward the beach, completely wrecking the sailors' intricate plan to hide everything by announcing her presence to whoever approached. The sunset scalawag might be the best mouser, but Special Lady had the brains of the family.

"I could live without seeing another vessel forever," she said. "I imagine Robin will stay here as well." She turned to me. "And what about you? If you must return to sailing life, I will of course go with you. There's no question about that."

The tightness in my chest began to loosen, and I could breathe again. "This place—here in this hollow—it's exactly where I want to be."

SOLDIERS FROM THE mainland came ashore and arrested all our sailors. Lucía, Tembe, Thomas, and the rest were taken to the ship in chains—all except Benjelloun. Once the others had been taken aboard, the girl marched down the path of her own accord, carrying her belongings and looking a bit smug. She stopped abruptly, glanced back at our tree, and saw Charles Sebastian standing at the edge of the hollow space watching her, with Special Lady and me curled behind. She gave us a curious glance, perhaps surprised by the unusual group of animals together. Then she came toward us and smiled sadly. She lifted her hand in a wave. "Farewell, friend mouse," she said. "I'm heading home, or so they say. Let's hope I make it." She hesitated, then added softly, "I admit I'm a little worried after what happened on my last voyage."

Charles Sebastian pointed his nose toward her and lifted his whiskers in farewell. "I'll miss you."

As Benjelloun turned and continued down the path to the sea, Charles Sebastian ran down the tree to the path and called out after her. "Benjelloun! It only takes one mouse to believe in you, and that one mouse is me!"

If she heard his squeaks, she didn't say so, but her shoulders straightened. She shifted the goods in her hands, then glanced back one last time with a small smile. "I really love that you and the cat are friends. I shall be thinking about that for a very long time." She hesitated awkwardly, then started walking again.

"Goodbye!" Charles Sebastian called after her. His voice wavered.

A moment later, the girl dipped her head to avoid a low-hanging branch, and then she was gone between the leaves.

* * *

CHARLES SEBASTIAN RETURNED to the hollow, more happy than sad about the fate of his friend, but still . . . the sad existed. Robin saw that we needed a moment, and he thoughtfully slid away to his own lair, where he preferred to be.

In the hours that followed, Special Lady and Charles

Sebastian and I listened as the human shouts and ship creaks gave way to gently lapping waves and the buzz of tree frogs. We nestled together, with the late-afternoon sun trickling between the leaves and warming our fur. The fear I'd carried all my life weighed just a little bit less now.

"The sails are engaged," reported the cat. "The vessel is moving away."

A lizard ran up our tree and peered at us, then darted away, but Special Lady was only mildly distracted by it. "The ship is growing smaller." She gave me a heartfelt look. "This feels . . . real. Doesn't it?"

I nodded, overcome with an unexpected wave of emotion.

Charles Sebastian caught my eye, and we touched noses, then snuggled in closer. The sun set over the sea, releasing a glorious burst of color in the sky.

"I can't see them anymore," Special Lady said finally. "They're gone."

And we were alone. We'd never felt so free. Special Lady was our cat now, and we were her mice. And we were staying here, together, in a new place called home.

Acknowledgments

If there's one thing a mouse needs, it's friends who believe in her.

The first person who believed in this book was my agent, Michael Bourret from Dystel, Goderich, & Bourret. Can you believe we've done 27 books together? I love working with you!

The next ones to believe in Clarice were Jennifer Klonsky and Ari Lewin at Putnam. Jen and I go way back—she bought my first book, *Wake*, in 2007. To be able to work together again is a dream come true. And then there's Ari the brave, a very special lady. The fact that someone with such a discerning eye wanted to edit my little mouse-mutiny book helped me believe we had an important story to tell. A special shout-out to assistant editor Elise LeMassena. Thank you so much for helping navigate my first book with Putnam.

What brings a story to life better than illustrations? Antonio Caparo, somehow you captured the images from my mind and brought them to life on these pages. I feel so lucky that you were willing to help tell Clarice's story.

Writing a book is only the beginning of a long journey. Producing it and getting it in the hands of readers takes a huge team effort. I offer my deepest thanks to the editing, design, marketing, publicity, sales, audio, and education and library teams at Putnam. Without you, *Clarice the Brave* would never have dared venture into the world. And to booksellers, teachers, librarians, and parents who hand this book to the readers in their lives: You have my heart.

Finally, to you. Thank you for opening this book and journeying across the seas with Clarice and Charles Sebastian and Special Lady and Benjelloun and me. It only takes one mouse to believe in you, dear reader, and that one mouse is me.